CHRISTMAS NIGHTS

A DIAMOND CREEK, ALASKA NOVEL

J.H. CROIX

This is a work of fiction. Names, characters, businesses, places, events and incidents are either the products of the author's imagination or used in a fictitious manner. Any resemblance to actual persons, living or dead, or actual events is purely coincidental.

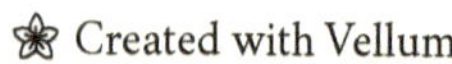 Created with Vellum

To new chapters in life even when we didn't know they were possible.

Sign up for my newsletter for information on new releases & get a FREE copy of one of my books!

http://jhcroixauthor.com/subscribe/

Follow me!
jhcroix@jhcroix.com
https://amazon.com/author/jhcroix
https://www.bookbub.com/authors/j-h-croix
https://www.facebook.com/jhcroix
https://www.instagram.com/jhcroix/

CHAPTER 1

The water enveloped her in its icy embrace. Janie Stevens felt the shock of it through every cell in her body. Fear raced through her as quickly as the cold surrounded her. Frantic, she kicked and struggled to swim to the surface, yet she felt instantly weighted down and weak. The rough current pulled at her, its power much greater than hers. Through the water, she could hear the muffled commotion around her. All she could think was she had to get to the surface and make sure Stella was safe. She kept struggling to gain momentum, getting weaker with every second. She was running out of oxygen, her lungs burning to breathe. She wanted to cry out, but she couldn't even take a breath.

Suddenly, a strong hand curled around her arm and yanked her up roughly. She gulped in air, swallowing salty ocean water along with her first breath. Coughing and sputtering, she opened her eyes and found herself staring into a pair of ocean blue eyes. A man she vaguely recognized was saying something, but she couldn't hear anything he said. All she cared about was finding out if her daughter was safe. She looked around frantically and saw the steel gray ocean roiled with choppy waves. Several boats were visible in the distance and bouncing in the rough waters. Her eyes landed on the boat she'd been in—it was listing badly to one side. "Stella, where's Stella?" she asked, struggling in the man's grip as he tugged her into a bright red heavy-duty raft.

"Stella's fine. She didn't fall overboard," the man said, gesturing behind them to the boats rocking in the waves.

Janie sat up and started to crawl back out of the boat. Not thinking clearly, she was determined to get to Stella. The man grabbed her arm and held tight. "Janie, hold still. See that boat there," he paused to point to another boat. "They're coming over to pick us up. Stella is safe, so don't put yourself in danger again by trying to swim to her. If you're not already hypothermic, you're damn close."

The fear pounding through her eased, but just barely. The combination of adrenaline, exhaustion and being colder than she'd ever been in her life muddled her thinking. She huddled in the raft and waited, shivering so hard, her teeth chattered. Time passed in a strange mix of fast and slow as she drifted in and out of awareness. Some indeterminate amount of time later, Janie woke up in a hospital bed. She started to get up immediately, kicking the covers back and spinning sideways.

"Mom! Stop! You're about to rip the IV out of your arm."

Janie froze and glanced toward the sound of her daughter's voice. Stella stood up from a chair in the corner. Her dark brown eyes were wide and concerned. She set a book down on the table beside the chair and walked to the bed. "Lay down and rest. You're stuck here for the night. The doctor already checked you in," Stella said with a half grin. At seventeen, Stella enjoyed bossing Janie around when she could.

Janie looked at Stella, intense relief coursing through her. The last thing she remembered was being terrified Stella might be in the same icy water she'd fallen into. They'd taken a late autumn trip across the bay for a last hike of the season. Kachemak Bay was beautiful in all seasons, but autumn was Stella's favorite time of year. Ever since Janie had adopted Stella three years ago, they went hiking spring, summer and autumn on the far side of Kachemak Bay. Diamond Creek, Alaska was situated on one side of the picturesque bay with several smaller communities on the other. This morning, they'd joined a group of various others crossing the bay by boat. On the way home, Stella had asked if she could ride in a different boat with some friends. Thinking nothing of it, Janie said yes.

She couldn't have known the clouds rolling in would rapidly kick up the wind and lead to a rough ride. Even then, she hadn't been worried. Born and raised in Diamond Creek, Janie was thoroughly accustomed to harsh weather. She still didn't know exactly what happened, but something had gone wrong with the boat she was riding in. Next thing she'd known, they'd been bailing water out of the boat, but hadn't been able to keep up. In what felt like seconds, the boat had started to sink. She remembered trying to grab onto the railing, but missed and splashed into the icy waters.

There was no safe time of year for a dip in the ocean in Alaska. Even at the height of summer, the ocean temperature didn't top sixty degrees Fahrenheit. In late October, the water was maybe forty degrees. Cold enough to lead to hypothermia within minutes. Janie looked over at Stella and sighed. She wasn't much for resting and certainly didn't enjoy feeling at the mercy of the doctor. Now that her almost drowning was over and there was no doubt Stella was safe, she would have to wait out the night in the hospital whether she wanted to, or not. She looked over at Stella who was watching her with a gleam in her eyes. Between her dark brown hair and eyes, Stella had the natural coloring for the look she preferred—an outdoorsy look with a hint of goth. At the moment, she had on her latest pair of chunky black glasses to go with her black painted nails. She wore a flannel shirt over a t-shirt and leggings paired with hiking boots. She eschewed makeup and certainly didn't need any with her creamy complexion, rosy cheeks and dark hair.

"I bet you're itching to jump out of bed and leave," Stella said with a slow grin.

Janie swung her legs back onto the bed, tugged the covers over her and threw a faux glare at Stella. She wasn't about to admit it, but she did feel tired and sore. "I'm fine. If I wanted to leave, I could. But, if the doctor thinks I need to stay, far be it from me to argue."

Stella's grin faded. "Dr. Marshall said you had hypothermia and wanted you here all night until your temperature was stable. I guess it was below ninety-three degrees and that's like a big deal. Are you warm now?"

Janie took in Stella's words and the worry in her voice and mentally scanned her body. She didn't feel warm, but she wasn't cold either. "I think I'm fine. How long have I been asleep?"

Stella shrugged. "I dunno. After Travis got you out of the water, they took you back on a different boat. By the time I got to the harbor, they'd already taken you away in an ambulance. They wouldn't let me switch boats because they had to rush everyone in who'd fallen in the water." She paused and took a gulping breath. "I was really scared when you fell in."

For Stella to say anything about being scared was huge. Stella was a sweet girl, but she'd been through a lot before she landed with Janie and carried herself with a wall of reserve. Janie knew if she commented on it, Stella would get quiet. So she let her heart absorb the small victory and reached over to squeeze Stella's hand resting on the edge of the bed. "I'm fine, just fine."

Stella gave her hand a return squeeze and tugged it free to twirl a lock of her hair around it, one of her preferred nervous habits. "Well, good. You're not allowed to fight with Dr. Marshall about leaving early though, okay?"

Janie rolled her eyes and leaned her head back. "Fine. Is everyone else okay?"

Stella nodded swiftly. "Oh yeah. A few other people fell in the water when you did, but everyone got fished out."

There was a soft knock at the door. Stella called out for whomever it was to come in. When the door swung open, Travis Wilkes stepped through. Janie suddenly realized the bright blue eyes she'd noticed when she was being pulled out of the water belonged to him.

He glanced between Stella and Janie. "Okay if I come in?"

Stella grinned. "I just said to come in."

Travis returned her smile. "That you did."

He strode toward the bed, and Janie felt suddenly self-conscious. Travis was a classic, rugged and handsome outdoorsman. He walked with the confidence with which he did everything. He was tall and nothing but muscle. On top of it all, he was an emergency responder, firefighter, save-everyone-who-needs-help kind of guy. She knew him in passing, but not well. He moved to Diamond Creek maybe five years prior and stirred all kinds of talk among the single women around town for a bit. In a small community like Diamond Creek, anyone new in town who wasn't a tourist might as well have a neon sign above them. With his brown hair gilded with gold, his blue eyes, and his strong, chiseled features, well, he was definitely easy on the eyes. He reached the side of the bed, his eyes coasting over her.

"How ya feeling?" he asked, a perfectly reasonable question under the circumstances.

Janie looked up at him and a jolt of electricity zipped through her. Men weren't something she paid much attention to because…well, just because. Hence, that little jolt took her off guard. Not to mention, he looked his usual rugged sexy self, while she was garbed in a voluminous pink polka-dotted hospital gown. She felt self-conscious and frumpy. She could only imagine how she looked after her impromptu dive into the ocean. Her hair felt tangled and messy.

She tried to recall if she'd ever been this close to him, save the blurry moments in the ocean when he yanked her out of the water. She'd laughed off the women she knew who had temporarily crushed on him, but she hadn't spent enough time with him to think much about him. Right now, with his eyes on her and his presence emanating strength, earthy sensuality and pure masculinity, well, she was all abuzz inside. Trying to cling to something that made her feel half-sane, she figured she must be out of it from almost drowning and still not thinking clearly.

Stella cued her into her lack of response to Travis. "Geez, Mom. You could at least tell him how you're doing. I mean, he saved your life."

Janie felt the blush race up her neck and cheeks and silently swore. "Oh sorry. I'm a little out of it. I think I'm doing fine. Stella told me Dr. Marshall wants me here for the night to make sure my temperature is back where it needs to be."

Travis nodded. "Probably a good idea. I checked your temp once we got off the water and you were below ninety-five, which means you were hypothermic. You look much better now." He reached over and casually rested the back of his hand on her forehead. "Feels about right now. Not a science, but a good guess," he said with a half-grin.

If she thought she'd felt a jolt before, his brief touch sent a prickle of awareness up her spine. A wash of heat suffused her, and her low belly fluttered when she met his eyes again. She managed a nod. "Well, that's good."

* * *

TRAVIS LOOKED DOWN into Janie's eyes, which he couldn't say he'd ever gotten close enough to see. He supposed they were hazel, but they were simply stunning. A soft green flecked with gold and nutmeg brown. Against her porcelain skin and glossy brown hair, they stood out. Her cheeks were stained pink, making him itch to let his hand slide down her cheek. He couldn't say why, but ever since he'd pulled her out of the water, she'd been hovering at the edges of his mind. He'd seen her around for years, but knew her only in passing. How he'd missed the fact that she was flat out gorgeous, he didn't know. This afternoon, during the windy ride back to Diamond Creek, he'd walked her into the small cabin on the boat and wrapped her in blankets. He'd sat with her and the others who were also dripping wet from their dip in the bay. In the course of his life, he'd sat with many people who'd been rescued from one situation or another and he'd never experienced the intense protectiveness he felt for her. Something about her called to him.

Disconcerted, he let his hand drop from her forehead, stepped back and slipped his hands into his pockets. "Well, just wanted to stop in and see how you were doing."

"Thank you for finding me and getting me out of the water," she said.

He shrugged. "No problem. Just glad I happened to be there. I was on the water taxi in front of you guys."

"Do you know what happened to the boat?"

"They're pretty sure the hull caught the edge of some rocks on the way out of the docks over there. Leak started slow and then once the waves picked up, it tore the hole wide enough to bring water in fast."

His mind spun back to the moment he'd tugged Janie into the raft. The second her eyes locked with his, all he'd known was he had to make sure she was safe. That was his job, but the feeling behind it was more than that, and he didn't quite know what to make of it.

She nodded slowly. "Thanks again. I don't remember much other than being dragged over the side of the raft."

Travis nodded, wrestling with the desire to remain in the room, but thinking it didn't fit given the low-key nature of their acquaintance. He caught Stella's eyes. "Make sure she stays warm." He gave a little wave and forced himself to leave the room.

CHAPTER 2

"Danny! Sit down. Now," Janie called, her tone edged with a gentle warning.

Danny Rivers immediately sat down. From the front of her first-grade classroom, Janie could see him practically vibrating in his seat. Danny tested her patience every day, but his saving grace was he was a sweet little boy. He had way too much energy and the classroom was an obstacle course for him. In her years of teaching, Janie had learned that the current world of education, one of testing and more testing, wasn't for every child. Danny loved to learn, but he was a tactile learner and needed to move around a lot more than she could allow for the most part. It was too distracting to the other kids. She tried to be as creative as she could with children like him, but some days, he just had to sit down and listen. Like today when someone from the fire station was coming to do their yearly talk about fire safety for the kids.

Janie scanned her small classroom—fifteen first graders, a hodgepodge of personalities who brought her so much joy. Danny was wiggling madly, but he was staying in his seat, so she took that as a win. "Okay kids! Our visitor today is a fireman, and we need to listen and ask good questions. Can we do that?"

Fifteen heads bobbed up and down. Janie smiled widely. "Awesome! Hold tight while I see if our visitor is here yet."

She stepped to the classroom doorway and glanced out, only to see Travis Wilkes striding down the hall beside the principal. Her breath hitched, her pulse rocketed, and her hand flew to her chest. Every year, the fire department sent someone here for these talks, but they never knew who it would be. She hadn't even considered it might be Travis. *Oh my God. Stop it. He's just a man. A really sexy man, but just a man. You're all weird because he kind of saved your life. It's like some weird bonding thing. It'll pass.* Her little pep talk didn't do much good when Travis and Principal Turner reached her.

"Janie, we have Travis Wilkes here today for the fire safety presentations. I was hoping you wouldn't mind being his guide for the day. I've asked one of our subs to sit in with your class after he's done here," Principal Turner said with a smile.

Janie knew she didn't have any choice in the matter. She liked her boss, she really did. Nancy Turner had been a teacher in Diamond Creek for twenty years before she became the principal. She navigated the political waters of running the school, while trying her best to advocate for funding and policies that supported the students and teachers. But right now, Janie really didn't want to be the gracious host for Travis. He made her pulse run wild and unsettled her inside. Yet, she knew it would seem odd if she tried to avoid it. She normally had no trouble behaving like a polite human, but Travis tongue-tied her. Like now, all she could do was nod. When Nancy's eyes narrowed, Janie realized she must seem off. With a mental shake, she nodded more firmly. "I've met Travis before. Nice to see you again," she said, catching his eyes, those damn gorgeous blue eyes. "I'd be happy to take him from class to class today."

"I'd love a guide. I'm solid on fire safety, but can't say I've ever known what to do with more than a few kids at a time," he said with a wry grin.

Nancy stepped back. "You're in good hands with Janie. I've got a meeting to get to. Thank you both." She spun on her heel and walked briskly down the hall.

Janie looked up at Travis. The moment his eyes locked with hers, her breath hitched and her pulse, which she'd barely gotten under control after the initial shock of seeing him, lunged again. She took a shaky breath and gestured to the door. "My class is one of the smallest, but you're starting with fifteen. That's five times more than a few."

Travis's mouth stretched in a slow grin. "I gotta admit, I'm damn glad you'll be with me. I had visions of kids running circles around me all day."

His uncertainty somehow eased her own wild anxiety. "How'd you end up doing this if kids make you nervous?" she asked.

"I lost the coin toss," he said with a shrug.

A laugh bubbled up. His rueful honesty was endearing. When she looked over, Travis's shoulders were shaking, his eyes glinting with mirth. "Laugh all you want. Little kids are a mystery to me."

"Come on. We'll start you off easy."

Without thinking, she slipped her hand in the crook of his elbow, which she instantly realized was a mistake. She could feel the corded muscles of his arm under her hand. His warmth and strength were like a pulsing power. Her entire body tightened. She knew it would seem strange if she yanked her hand away, so she decided to bluster through the moment. She tugged him through the door into her classroom. Just as they stepped inside, Danny sprung up from his seat. "Watch! I can run to Ms. Stevens' desk and..."

She released Travis' arm. "Danny! Back in your seat. We all know you can race to my desk and back super fast."

Danny froze and spun in her direction. He looked so tempted to finish what he'd set out to do. She could practically see the little wheels turning in his brain. His eyes landed on Travis. "Hey! Are you a firefighter?"

Travis glanced to Janie. While Danny might not have cued in to her warning, Travis did. He kept silent, his lips quirking when she looked to Danny again.

"Danny, of course he's a firefighter. You already knew that. You have two choices: sit down right now and get to stay for his talk, or take a time out for three minutes in the back."

Danny scurried to his desk, his brown hair flopping over his forehead when he sat down and wiggled his bottom in place for emphasis.

* * *

TRAVIS FOLLOWED Janie to the next classroom of wild children, marveling at her ease with them. She accompanied him to ten classrooms by the end of the day. Danny, the little boy who could barely sit still in her class, remained the most amusing highlight of the day with his antics. He'd asked question upon question, ending with another offer to show Travis how fast he could run to Janie's desk. Janie adroitly managed all of the children throughout the day with a mixture of warmth and firm guidance.

He was at the end of the last presentation in a second grade class. He'd moved on to questions with Janie calling on various children whose hands flew up.

"You're up, Nate," Janie called, gesturing to a little boy who almost matched Danny with his wiggling in his seat.

Nate smiled and looked from Janie to Travis. "How many fires do you put out a week?" he asked.

Travis tapped his index finger on his chin and shrugged. "It's different every week. Sometimes the fire station goes weeks without responding to an actual fire. Remember, we're emergency responders too, so we get called to all kinds of emergencies, not just fires."

Nate nodded solemnly and bit the inside of his cheek. His eyes bounced from Travis to Janie and back again. "Do you like Ms. Stevens?"

His next question startled Travis, both that Nate

asked such a question and that he was so prescient. Because the truth was spending a whole day with Janie was testing the limits of his control. It was safe to say Travis liked Janie... a lot. An elementary school was a decidedly not good place to have the hots for anyone, but Travis's body had been on notice all day around Janie. Her dark hair was pushed back behind a headband with her hazel eyes bright. She was dressed practically in jeans and a button down blouse. Her curvy body filled out her jeans. He had to remind himself to keep his eyes away from the shadowed valley between her generous breasts. By no means were they on display, but there wasn't much she could do unless she wore a giant bag to hide her lush curves. He felt heat rise within, the whip of lust lashing at him, and tried to ignore it.

He could feel Janie's gaze on him. He gathered himself and met Nate's gaze, which held a small gleam. "Of course I like Ms. Stevens. Don't you?" he countered, aiming for a casual tone in his response.

Nate nodded emphatically. "She was my favorite teacher last year!"

Janie chuckled and arched a brow. "I bet you love Mrs. Davis this year too, right?"

Another emphatic nod from Nate, and Janie promptly called on the last hand held high. Not much later, she walked Travis down the hall. "Do you need to check in with Principal Turner before you go?" she asked.

"Don't think so. She said she'd be in meetings the rest of the day."

Janie nodded and kept walking until they reached the main entrance to the school. "Well, you're done. You'd better get going before the last bell rings.

Between the buses and the stampede of kids, you might get trapped."

She looked up at him when she spoke. He heard her words, but didn't quite absorb them. All he could think about was what it might be like to kiss her bright pink lips. Her lips were as lush as the rest of her. She had a small dimple in the center of her bottom lip, and he wanted… Holy hell. He wanted all kinds of things, every single one of them absolutely naughty given where they were. He looked down into her hazel eyes and his question surprised him.

"Don't suppose I could take you out to dinner?"

Her breath hitched, her lips parting just slightly, and her eyes widened. For a few beats, she didn't speak. She gave her head a little shake. "Um, I…" Another shake of her head. "I suppose…yes." Her last word came out with force, and she looked startled once she spoke.

He didn't care to ponder her hesitation at the moment. "Okay, how about tomorrow night?"

"Tomorrow?" Her eyes were still wide and surprise lingered in them.

"For dinner."

She held still for another long moment before nodding slowly. "Okay. Um, I don't…" She paused and took a deep breath, a look of resignation passing over her face. "I don't really date much. Should I give you my number or something? Should I meet you somewhere?"

"How about you give me your number, and I'll pick you up?"

Her creamy cheeks went pink. "Okay." She quickly recited her number, which he punched into his phone. He sensed she might back out, so he didn't want to give her time to do so.

"Okay, I'll call you tomorrow afternoon." The bell rang, and he gave a wave. "I'd better run."

Once he was outside, he jogged down the stairs and to his truck. He turned to look at the entrance and saw Janie standing there, looking out through the glass doors.

CHAPTER 3

"Stella! Where's your homework?" Janie called out as she strode through the kitchen.

She heard a door open and close and then footsteps pounding down the stairs. Stella sprinted off the bottom of the stairs and past Janie. "I'm doing it now!" she declared as she skidded to a stop by her backpack sitting on a bench by the kitchen door.

Janie continued past the stairs to the laundry room. Her home was a cozy Cape style home. She purchased it before she adopted Stella, but she'd always had an extra bedroom because she'd been a foster parent for several years before Stella landed with her. She liked her house because the downstairs was more open than most Cape homes. The staircase was centered in the middle of the downstairs with the kitchen and dining room on one side and a living room on the other. The area connecting the garage to the home held a bathroom and laundry room. There were no walls separating the rooms with the staircase serving as a natural divider. Tall windows were along every wall and offered a view of Kachemak Bay from the hillside where the home was situated above downtown Diamond Creek.

Stella had been placed with Janie in foster care on a rainy winter night. She'd been removed from her father's care not long after her mother died of an accidental heroin overdose. Before she'd been placed in foster care, Stella's parents had been well known to child protection. There had been years of reports about drug abuse and the condition of the home. After Stella's mother died, her father didn't lift a finger to change things and drifted in and out of jail. He didn't fight Stella's removal and never once showed up in court for the hearings. Janie had taken one look at Stella with her guarded brown eyes and felt her heart crack open—all she wanted was to make sure Stella knew she deserved to be loved. At first, Stella was a bit like a cactus—prickly and bristly. She'd slowly warmed up. When Stella's state social worker asked Janie if she'd be willing to adopt Stella, there had been absolutely no hesitation for Janie. She loved Stella through and through, and wanted nothing more than to make sure Stella knew family was what you made it. It took Stella months to decide she wanted to be adopted. Without her therapist there to help her walk through it, Janie wasn't sure Stella could have allowed herself to believe anyone could love her.

Janie pulled the laundry out of the washer and tossed it in the dryer before returning to the kitchen. Stella was leaning over the counter, her feet hooked around the legs of a stool as she carefully completed math problems. The deal with homework was it had to be done by five in the evening. Janie had quickly discovered Stella needed clear expectations to get anything done. The first six months or so, she'd fought against any expectation because she'd never had them. Yet, now she generally went along with them. Janie didn't nag, but expected Stella's completed homework to be in a folder at the end of the counter. If it wasn't there, Janie checked with Stella.

Janie gave Stella's shoulder a squeeze as she stepped past her to the stove where she put a teakettle on to boil. While Stella quietly completed her homework, Janie prepped a quick dinner of salmon pie, a favorite of Stella's. While she cooked, Janie's mind wandered to Travis. Well, if she was being honest, she'd had a hard time *not* thinking about him after spending most of the day with him. Watching him graciously field inquisitive, random, and occasionally silly questions from kids all day long had only endeared him to her. Aside from the fact he was a quintessential rugged, sexy guy, he was kind and patient even when he sometimes looked as if he wanted to run and hide. She had no idea what to do about the fact she'd agreed to have dinner with him. She hadn't been on a date in years. She tried to remember the last date she'd had and kept coming up blank.

She didn't tend to think about men because it made her think too much about her own past. With a mental shake, she focused her attention on pinching the edges of the pastry around the small pies. Half of her wanted to back out of dinner with Travis, while the other half of her was all but stomping its feet at that idea. *It's about damn time you went on a date. You can't keep letting the past hold you back. Not all men are bad.* She physically shook her head, trying to shove those thoughts away. A problem she hadn't considered was what to tell Stella. Conveniently, tomorrow night was piano recital practice for Stella, and she was already planning to spend the night at a friend's house afterwards. Janie could easily have her dinner date and never bother to mention it to Stella. Yet, Janie didn't want to avoid what should be an open topic.

She slid the salmon pies into the oven and set the timer. Stella put her pencil down and slipped her homework into its folder. "Guess I don't need to bother leaving this here since you saw me do it, huh?" Stella asked with a grin.

"Nah. Go ahead and put it in your backpack."

Stella quickly stuffed the folder in her backpack and returned to her stool, spinning in a slow circle on it. "Parker wants to take me to the Christmas Dance. I told him I didn't know because it's not like he's my boyfriend or anything. We're just friends."

Stella was referring to Parker Schmidt, a friend who was in the high school band with her. Stella played piano and Parker played drums. He'd befriended Stella at school before she found her place in the small circle of friends she had. Janie had met Parker and his parents many times and trusted him. Her guess was Parker liked Stella as more than a friend, but Stella took skittish to great lengths, hardly able to believe someone could like her that way. So, they were technically friends.

Janie looked over at Stella who was still spinning her stool slowly. "Dances like that are more fun with friends anyway. If you're asking me if you should go with him, I say yes. You'll have fun."

Stella stopped spinning and twirled a purple lock

of hair around her finger. Janie had helped her dye it with streaks of purple last night. Stella chewed on bottom lip and stared at Janie. "I've never been to a dance like that. What if it's all weird?"

Janie angled her head to the side and shrugged. "Hard to know what it'll be like unless you go. If you go with Parker, you'll probably have fun. Are any of your other friends going?"

Stella nodded, still twirling her hair. "Uh huh. I'll think about it."

Janie bit back a grin. If Stella was willing to think about it, that meant she wanted to go. "Okay. If you decide to go, don't forget to tell me when it is."

Stella grinned and nodded. "Got it."

Janie took a breath and shifted gears. "Speaking of things like this, I, uh, might be going on a dinner date." She managed to get the words out without sounding as foolish as she felt.

Stella dropped her hand from her hair, her eyes widening. "Really? Mom, you should totally go. You never date. Who is it?"

Stella's excited response startled Janie. "You think I should go? I'm not even sure if..."

"Of course you should go! My friends always ask how come you're not with anyone. You're pretty and nice and all that. So who is it?"

Janie fought the flush spreading up her cheeks. "Okay, I wasn't sure how you might feel about it. You come first, so thinking about dating means thinking about how it fits into our lives."

Stella waved her hand dismissively. "Fine, fine. It's just a date. Who is it?" she asked, leaning over the counter.

"It's Travis Wilkes," Janie finally said.

Stella's eyes widened and a slow grin spread across her face. "I knew it! When he came to see you in the hospital, it was so obvious he thought you were cute."

Janie rolled her eyes, although her mind was spinning with Stella's casual comment. "Whatever. Anyway, I just wanted to let you know. I'm still not sure about it."

Stella returned the eye roll with emphasis. "Whatever. Maybe you need to go talk to a therapist. You made me go forever. It shouldn't be such a thing to decide if you're going out to dinner with someone. Travis is nice, he's totally hot and he saved your life," Stella declared with another spin on her stool.

Janie laughed, but she turned away, swallowing against the tightness in her chest. Stella's casual observation that it shouldn't be a thing was right on point. Except Stella didn't know Janie's past. The little buzz of excitement she felt fizzled slightly at the thought. Janie busied herself getting plates out and pouring water for each of them, filling the time until the oven buzzer went off.

* * *

TRAVIS TOOK a gulp of coffee and sighed. He leaned his hips against the counter in the break room at the fire station and glanced at the clock. It was barely past eight in the morning, and the crew had just finished dealing with a residential fire on the outskirts of town. Unsurprisingly, the fire had started in the kitchen after a busy mother forgot to turn a burner off. Aside from a badly damaged kitchen, no one was hurt, which was a win as far as Travis was concerned.

"Hey there."

Travis glanced up at the sound of Sylvia Cunning-ham's voice. "Hey Sylvia! Thanks for getting a fresh pot of coffee ready," he said with a lift of his paper coffee cup.

Sylvia stepped into the break room, her eyes scanning over Travis. "You don't look any worse for wear. How'd it go?"

"Fire's out and no one's injured."

Sylvia grinned. "Well, we can be glad the daily emergency is already out of the way."

Sylvia was the administrative assistant at the police and fire station. Her husband had been the police chief for years, but he'd retired after a back injury. Sylvia stayed on and essentially ran the station for all intents and purposes. She was the official mother hen for the entire police force and fire crew. She was steady as a rock, warm and kind. She declared she had no intention of retiring until she couldn't work anymore. Her looks matched her personality with her round figure, twinkling blue eyes and graying hair.

Travis chuckled at her comment. "You're right. Guess we've had our daily emergency already." He took another long swallow of coffee. "Damn good coffee. Just what I needed. I meant to snag some earlier, but the call came in while I was driving here, so I'm low on caffeine at the moment."

Sylvia winked. "Drink up. I'm headed back up front. Tell the guys I'm ordering pizza for everyone for lunch."

"Thanks Sylvia!" Travis called as she walked briskly out of the room and down the hall.

After he downed his cup of coffee and refilled it, he strode to the windows and looked out. It was hard to find a place without a view in Diamond Creek, and the fire station had one as well. Its back wall looked out over Kachemak Bay. The water glittered under the bright sun, its surface choppy from the wind scudding across it. There were a few boats out, rocking in the water. With winter approaching, there were far fewer boats out than at the height of summer. Travis recalled last week when he'd pulled Janie out of the water. A fluke had quickly sunk the boat she'd been riding in. He was relieved a few other boats had been around to help because otherwise the day might have turned out quite differently.

Late that afternoon, he jogged down the steps of the fire station and over to his truck. The air was scented with impending snow. Travis climbed in his truck and zoomed home. He lived in one half of a duplex in downtown Diamond Creek. He didn't spend much time at home with work often taking him out of town. Aside from his regular job as a firefighter for Diamond Creek, he took pick up jobs on hot shot crews that flew into fires in remote areas, and he was also a fisherman. Juggling multiple jobs was part of life in Alaska with the weather and seasons leading to fluctuating needs. He raced into his apartment to shower and change. He was on his way to pick up Janie for dinner. When he called to confirm today, he sensed hesitation from her, but he barreled through it. He couldn't stop thinking about her hazel eyes and lush curves. He wasn't sure what it was about her, but she made him want all kinds of things. His life didn't leave much room for dating, so he kept things casual. Nothing about Janie felt casual. Aside from the pounding lust she elicited, she made him want to wrap her in his arms and hold her close.

Once she gave him her address, he knew right where her place was. She lived on the hillside above town on a winding road. He slowed when he saw the mailbox with her house number on it and turned into the driveway to find a charming cape home sitting at the end. The view of the bay spread out behind the home. It was early evening, but the sun was already setting, streaking the sky with lavender and pink.

Before he reached the door, it swung open. Janie stood in the doorway. A gust of wind blew past her, sending her dark hair in a swirl. She ran a hand through the disordered locks and glanced up at him. "Hi," she said simply.

She wore jeans and a fitted tank top with a silky blouse over it. It was simple enough, yet insanely tempting because her breasts stretched the fabric of her tank top. Travis's fingers itched to reach over and trace along the curves. He forced his eyes up to find her cheeks pinkening. That sent another lash of lust through him. He cleared his throat. "Hey. You ready to go?"

At her nod, he took a step back, making room for her to step onto the small porch. When she turned to lock the door behind her, her scent drifted to him—a subtle blend of vanilla and honey. Somehow, he kept a leash on his body and managed to walk down the stairs and to his truck. Once he was seated beside her, he glanced her way and was startled at the look on her face. Fear glimmered in the depths of her layered hazel eyes. He had been about to start his truck, but he froze and lowered his hand.

CHAPTER 4

"Are you okay?" Travis asked, his eyes coasting over her face.

Janie swallowed against the tightness in her throat and nodded, swatting back the feelings she hadn't expected to rise up right now. "Oh yeah, I'm fine." She tried to inject a breeziness in her tone, but it came out flat. On the heels of the old fear she thought she'd chased away long ago rose embarrassment. All she'd done was climb in his truck, and he seemed to notice she felt a little off. She took a breath and let it out slowly. "Where are we going?" she asked, hoping to move the conversation along normal topics.

He held her gaze for another beat and then seemed to accept her shift in topic. "Thought I'd leave it up to you."

"Oh. Hmm. Maybe you can tell me a few places you like and we'll go from there? I'm pretty easy to please when it comes to food."

He shrugged. "The Brewery or the Boathouse?"

"The Brewery then. I haven't been there in a while."

Travis headed down the hill to Diamond Creek, making small talk along the way. He had to pause and wait for a mama moose and her two calves to meander across the road. Janie couldn't hold back a small laugh when one of the calves paused to turn and sniff the truck's bumper.

"I'd rather have my bumper meet them this way than the other option," Travis said with a chuckle.

After the calf completed its investigation of Travis's bumper, it jogged to catch up with its mother, all gangly legs as it made it way to the far side of the road. Travis slowly rolled past the trio and turned onto the road where Diamond Creek Brewery was. When they walked in a few minutes later, Janie scanned the space. Although the height of tourist season had passed, the brewery was busy. She saw a few acquaintances, but no close friends. She gave a silent sigh of relief. Gossip was a foregone conclusion in Diamond Creek. It was her hometown and she loved it, but rumors tended to take off like brush fire here. Considering that she couldn't even recall the last time she'd been on a date, if anyone happened to notice that's what she was doing with Travis, well, there would be gossip.

Janie was surprised to find dinner passed quickly and easily despite her internal awkwardness. Travis was easy to be around, and the brewery afforded a comfortable environment. The brewery was housed in a refurbished plane hanger, a far cry from its original state with model planes hanging from the ceiling, brightly colored rugs and curtains lending a warmth to the airy space. She found herself watching Travis with an alertness that startled her. Time and again, she couldn't help the lunge of her pulse when his mouth curled up on one side. While he was an excellent example of, well, pure manliness between his fit, muscled body and chiseled features, an edge of humor softened him. Over a few too many glasses of wine, she learned he'd been born and raised in Anchorage, his parents and his brother were still in Anchorage, and he'd learned how to fish in his family's commercial fishing business. He'd branched out on his own when he moved to Diamond Creek. He still fished, but claimed he'd never wanted that to be his only job. Commercial fishing, by its nature, was beset by fluctuating income, risky work, and uncertainty.

"I usually crew on a few salmon runs every year, but that's it. That way, I can actually enjoy fishing and not worry if it's a bad year," he offered with a shrug.

Janie enjoyed another sip of the brewery's delicious gooseberry wine. "Smart move. I've seen many people go through some tough years when fishing runs are down."

"Exactly. Anyway, your family is here in Diamond Creek, right?" he asked.

"Oh yeah, the whole lot," she said with a laugh. "Actually, for my immediate family, it's just me and my mom. My dad died in a fishing accident when I was little…"

"Oh, I'm sorry," Travis said quickly.

"Thank you, but it's okay. I miss him, but it's been twenty years. I've had lots of time to get used to it. Anyway, my mom's family's pretty big though. She has two sisters and two brothers and most of them are still in Diamond Creek. When I adopted Stella, she was a little overwhelmed with all the attention."

"I can imagine. She's a good kid. She was pretty worried about you after your dip in the bay a few weeks ago."

Janie smiled, warmth blooming in her chest. "Stella's great. She had fun fussing over me for a day or two."

At that moment, their waitress arrived to clear the table. Once she'd stacked their empty plates on her tray, she glanced between them. "Coffee or dessert?"

Travis glanced to Janie and arched a brow. Just that little gesture, and Janie felt distracted. The blue of his eyes was so bright. She mentally shook herself and looked up at the waitress. "Coffee would be great."

Travis followed suit and they waited quietly while their waitress threaded her way toward the kitchen in the back. Janie felt Travis's gaze on her and flushed. She wasn't used to being noticed. She was who she was—an independent, single mother too busy to think about dating. She knew just about all the locals in Diamond Creek to some extent and was known in return. She couldn't say she'd consciously cultivated a 'stay away' vibe when it came to men, but she had enough sense to know she didn't exactly invite attention. Hence, she was firmly in the friend category. She wasn't much interested in flings, so she avoided the hordes of temporary residents in the summer. That's why Travis stood out to so many women when he moved to Diamond Creek—he was new and he wasn't just passing through.

She forced herself to glance up and found his gaze still upon her. She had to fight not to look away. She was awash in uncertainty, mostly because this was a situation she generally didn't allow to happen. She thrived on feeling strong and confident in her life, but her life didn't include a smoking hot man looking across the table with desire flashing in his eyes. Heat rolled through her, and her breath caught. Her mind blanked and she forgot her usual worries—about trust, about the wreckage the wrong man could leave behind.

The moment was snapped when the waitress delivered their coffees. Not much later, her mind slightly less muddled with desire, she walked alongside Travis out of the brewery. His palm rested on her low back, the heat searing through her lightweight down jacket. When they stepped outside, snow was falling softly—light, fluffy flakes floating down and glittering in the lights from the brewery.

* * *

TRAVIS DROVE through the falling snow. He was relieved it was light because his concentration was weak at the moment. The simple act of sitting across from Janie had driven him to the edge of his restraint. Her rich brown hair, her porcelain skin with her cheeks flushed and those eyes of hers, swirling with layers of color, had nearly undone him. He was still marveling at the fact he'd somehow managed to never get close enough to her to realize she was stunning. She was also intelligent with a sly sense of humor and independent. It was clear she was entirely accustomed to relying on herself for just about everything. Oddly enough, it made him long to be someone she could lean on.

The space inside his truck was humming. He was

so attuned to her presence that he felt every subtle shift of her body. When he pulled into her driveway and rolled to a stop, he didn't wait and climbed out quickly, walking around to open the passenger door. She'd started to turn sideways when he swung the door open. Her eyes widened and a little laugh escaped. "Oh, I didn't know anyone opened doors anymore."

He shrugged. "I do," he said simply.

Her jacket was unzipped, and his eyes fell of their own accord to the shadowed valley between her breasts. When he realized he was staring, he forced his eyes up, noticing the flutter of her pulse in her neck. Without thinking, he leaned forward, stopping a whisper away from her lips. Though it took every ounce of discipline he had, he needed to give her the chance to turn away. Her hazel eyes caught his. He saw nothing but desire there. When he held still for another breath, she leaned forward and closed the tiny distance between them.

The moment her lips met his, need jolted through him. Her lips were soft and warm, a contrast to the cold air and snow swirling around them. For a second, he felt tension running through her, but she sighed and it dissolved. He stepped closer into the small gap of space. With her turned sideways on the passenger seat, he stepped between her knees and angled his head to the side. On another breath, her lips parted and he swept his tongue inside. He nearly growled with relief and claimed her mouth. After a second's hesitation, she met him stroke for stroke, her tongue tangling with his. He threaded a hand into her silky hair and dove into the warmth and sweetness of her. He couldn't have said what he expected her to kiss like, but it wasn't this—this wild abandon of kisses, nips, and strokes of her tongue.

He curled an arm around her waist, pulling her close against him. The feel of her soft curves against him whipped the lash of lust yet again, and he tore his lips free. He needed to taste her and trailed kisses along her jawline and the column of her throat. A soft moan came from her, and it was all he could do not to yank her shirt down and suck one of her taut nipples in his mouth. She suddenly tensed against him. He lifted his head to find headlights angling in their direction from the driveway.

"Oh! Someone's here," she said, her voice lilting high. She glanced up, her eyes wide and her lips plump from his kisses.

Travis yanked on the reins of need and forced himself to take a step back. He slowly loosened his hand in her hair and slid his fingers through it as he stepped back again. "Expecting someone?" he asked.

She shook her head. His eyes, which seemed to be entirely out of his control, dipped down and landed on her nipples, which were straining against her tank top. Holy hell. He didn't know what it was about her, but it was all he could do not to yank her back to him and dive right back into their kiss. He gulped in the cold air and glanced over to see the car rounding the curve of her circular driveway.

A figure climbed out and waved. "Hey Travis!"

Janie nudged him in the leg with her knee. "It's Stella," she whispered fiercely. "Let me..."

He stepped back before she finished, and she leapt out of his truck. He experienced a physical pang to have her move away. With a hard shake of his head, he closed the passenger door and tucked his hands in his jacket pockets, following Janie slowly.

"Hey hon, I thought you were spending the night with Kayla," Janie said as she met Stella on her approach.

"I was supposed to, but she's got a stomach thing. She was fine earlier, but now she's throwing up. Her mom came to get her from recital and offered to take me home on the way." Stella glanced past Janie to Travis and gave a little wave.

"Hey Stella, how's it going?" he asked, striving for a casual tone.

He was still mentally redirecting his body. A single kiss, and he felt like he was on fire, lust galloping through him. But right here, right now, Janie's daughter was busy chattering about how much she didn't want to catch whatever her friend had. Janie stepped past Stella and approached the car to speak through the window.

Travis had reached Stella's side by then, and she glanced over with a smile. "How was dinner?"

He was unaccustomed to teenage daughters querying him about dates, but he gamely went along with her question. "Dinner was great. How was recital?"

Stella shrugged. "Boring. I've got my part down, so mostly I play it over and over while a few others are still trying to nail their parts."

Janie gave a wave and stepped away from the car, which slowly eased past his truck in the drive and made its way back to the road. Janie reached their side and opened her mouth to speak, but Stella cut in. "We should have Travis in for hot chocolate, Mom."

"Uh, well, I don't know if Travis..."

When Janie glanced to him, her eyes questioning, he nodded quickly. He wasn't ready to give up any time with her. "I'd love to," he said quickly. When Stella flashed a grin at him, he bit back the urge to laugh. He couldn't say why, but he sensed he had an ally in her.

CHAPTER 5

*J*anie brushed the snow off her windshield and tapped the snowbrush on her tire, knocking the loose snow off. She climbed in her car and turned the heat down. Stella had started her car for her a while ago on her way to get on the bus. Janie paused to look beyond the house. Kachemak Bay sparkled under the bright sunshine. The snowstorm last night had dropped close to a foot of snow and cleared out before morning. The mountains on the far side of the bay were stark against the sky, their white peaks towering high over the water. She took a deep breath and let it out slowly. She'd barely slept last night. After Travis had kissed her senseless and then stayed for hot chocolate with her and Stella, her mind ran laps most of the night—obsessing over just what the hell she'd been thinking by kissing him.

Just because you've been avoiding men for years doesn't mean you should keep doing it. It's not worth it, that's why.

You know perfectly well not all men are anything like your mom's ex. Stop letting the past call the shots.

She shook her head, trying to knock her mind off its back and forth chatter. She had one very good reason for avoiding men. After her father died, her mother got involved with Randy Price. He was charming and solicitous at first. Within six months, he'd moved in with them and Janie was struggling to accept the possibility her mother might get married again. She'd adored her father and had been devastated when he died in a fishing accident in the Bering Sea during crab season. She didn't actively dislike Randy at first, but it was hard to accept the role he played in her mother's life and, by extension, hers. After Randy had been living with them for a while, things slowly started to change—the pace was so gradual, nothing was obvious until it was too late. Next thing she knew, her mother rarely left the house and isolated herself from her friends. Randy constantly made belittling comments about her mother's appearance, her cooking, her cleaning and just about everything. Janie watched her strong, confident and independent mother become a shadow of herself. The man who'd seemed to be caring and loving was anything but.

Janie had been worried about her mother, but she had no idea what to do about it. There were a few times she heard them argue. Bruises showed up every so often on her mother, and her mother always had a quick excuse for how they happened, even once when her eye was swollen shut. She claimed she'd slipped on the ice and collided with the door handle on her car.

Janie was in her early teens by then and, as was

often the case, was testing the limits left and right. One afternoon, she talked back to Randy when he complained about her mother's cooking. He'd looked over at her, his eyes cold, and then stood up, punching her where she sat at the table. Hard. Janie's chair had toppled over, and she'd curled up on the floor, pain shooting through her jaw where his fist had connected. Her mother stormed across the kitchen and threw a cast iron pan at Randy. He fell like a stone. Janie was the one who called the police and held her mother while she cried. She'd watched while it took her mother several years to make it back to the strong woman she'd once been.

The subsequent trial had been grueling. Even though he'd broken Janie's jaw and she'd been willing to testify, Randy had fought the charges relentlessly. Janie had learned the hard way how little the courts supported women and children in cases such as that. Since her mother had avoided filing charges on him again and again, there was little official history for Randy's abusive behavior. He claimed to have learned from past offenses with an ex-girlfriend and had been a model participant in an anger management group. Eventually, he was convicted and sentenced to a puny six months in prison. As soon as he got out, he was back in town and tried again and again to woo her mother back. She managed to hold her ground, but it wore on her. He was arrested yet again when Janie came home to witness him knock her mother out on the front porch. This time, he was sentenced to a full year, which still seemed pathetic to Janie. He hadn't returned to Diamond Creek in the years since, but Janie kept tabs on him. The last she knew, he was living in Fairbanks and had added to his list of arrests for domestic violence with another girlfriend.

The view had gone hazy in front of her as she thought about why she'd generally avoided men like the plague. Randy had seemed nice at first. She didn't trust herself to know if someone was out to fool her just like her mother had been fooled. It had nearly destroyed her mother. Until Travis, no man had tempted her to bother trying. With a shake, she forced her mind to the moment. She needed to get to work.

That evening, she sat in the back of the high school auditorium while Stella gamely played through another piece during recital practice. Piano had turned out to be a saving grace for Stella. She was naturally gifted and loved playing. It was the one activity Janie had managed to nudge Stella into during the first few years after she'd started staying with Janie. Stella had been socially awkward and shy, preferring to be invisible back then. She was still on the shy side, but piano lessons and her subsequent participation in band at school had helped her find friends and gave her something to be proud of.

Janie and a few other mothers took turns carpooling for the kids in recital practices, and tonight was her turn. She used the time to grade homework and plan assignments out for her classes. She finished one stack of spelling homework and slipped it into a folder.

"Hey Janie," someone said.

She glanced up at the sound of her name and grinned when she saw Ginger Sanders sidling her way down the narrow aisle. Ginger was a speech therapist at school with her. They often took lunches together.

Ginger's straight dark hair was tied back with a bright red ribbon.

She plunked down beside Janie with an elaborate sigh, her blue eyes twinkling when she glanced to Janie. "Grading homework, huh?"

Janie nodded. "Of course. I usually get all caught up when I'm on carpool duty. What brings you here?"

"We had to schedule a few planning meetings for some kids, and Principal Turner decided we should do them after school." Ginger rolled her eyes and shook her head. "I've worked with Nancy for years, but it's always driven me nuts that she wants to do things after hours."

Janie returned the eye roll. "I know. God love her, but the few times I've been stuck doing that, we're there for hours."

Ginger nodded emphatically. "Exactly! It's almost eight o'clock! Anyway, when I was passing by, I saw you hiding back here, so I thought I'd pop in. What's up?"

"The usual. You know how busy it's been at school. Between that and Stella, that's my life." As she made the comment, she realized how true it rang. That was her life—work and her daughter. She loved her job and loved Stella to pieces. When she'd become a foster parent, she hoped to simply be able to be there for children passing through rough times. She never forgot that if she hadn't had a mother who stood up for her and a family to rely on, she might very well have ended up in a similar situation because of Randy. Yet, she hadn't counted on Stella landing in her lap and almost instantly crawling into her heart. Adopting Stella brought so much to her, and she felt so enriched by how their family had come to be. Yet, beyond that and her own family and friends, her world was a small circle. Travis, who seemed permanently camped in the edges of her mind now, strode boldly front and center.

Ginger arched a brow, yet remained silent.

"What?" Janie asked, crossing her legs and absently fiddling with the stack of papers on the small tray.

"I know it's never fun to be a topic of gossip, but rumor has it you were at dinner with Travis Wilkes at the brewery the other night," Ginger said, barely suppressing a smile.

Janie felt her cheeks heat and silently swore. "Are you serious?"

Ginger nodded and bit her lip. "Would I lie?"

Janie sighed and shook her head. "So what if I was?"

Ginger slapped her hand on the armrest of her seat. "Oh my god! You had a date and you didn't tell me. And not just a date, but dinner with Travis Wilkes who's eye candy to half the damn town."

Janie figured her cheeks were practically glowing at this point. "It was just dinner. That's all." *Yeah, dinner and a kiss to die for.*

Ginger leaned back, her eyes sobering. "Look, I figured you'd rather hear the gossip from me than someone else. You gave me the same respect back when I started seeing Cam. You don't really date, so I kinda thought you might actually like him. All joking aside, Travis is a solid guy. Cam knows him pretty well because he's one of the back up first responders for the ski lodge if Cam or Gage aren't available. Don't feel like you have to explain yourself to me, but you know you'll hear about it from Becky Wright, so..."

Becky was another teacher at the elementary school. Although she was married and had been for years, she loved drooling over single men and tended to trade in gossip just like this. Janie took a slow breath and wrinkled her nose when she looked over at Ginger. "Right. Of course. If you heard about it, Becky probably knows more about my dinner date than I do."

Ginger grinned and shrugged. "She knows what crazy story she's concocted. Anyway, at least tell me if you like him."

Janie glared at her and then shrugged. "Look, it's the first date I went on in I don't know how long. He's a nice guy, and he's..." She paused, another wash of heat rolling through her, this one something quite different from embarrassment. The memory of his lips on hers sent desire spinning inside and heat sliding through her veins.

"He's hot is what he is. I mean, he's not for me, but he could be for you," Ginger offered with a wink.

Janie laughed softly. "It was just dinner. Okay?"

"Yeah, but you don't really do dinner. He dates here and there, but it's nothing more than way casual." Ginger paused, her eyes narrowing. "Are you okay?"

On the heels of the unfamiliar desire Travis elicited, Janie felt anxious. She wasn't used to this. She liked feeling in control. She didn't like how Travis affected her. For crying out loud, he was nowhere near her right now, and she was thrumming with a need she'd never experienced before, which made her feel out of control and all at the whim of a man. She forced herself to take a breath and caught Ginger's eyes. "I'm not so used to anything to do with men. I'm a little freaked out I even went to dinner with him. Maybe it seems crazy..."

Ginger shook her head quickly and leaned sideways to pull her into a hug. "We all have pasts and they mess with our heads. You don't have to talk about it unless you want to, but don't beat yourself up. I didn't talk about it much, but I was all kinds of crazy in my head when I started falling for Cam. If you want to talk, just say so and I'm here."

The tightness in Janie's chest eased at Ginger's words. She wasn't ready to talk just now, but she appreciated Ginger's no-nonsense, completely non-judgmental support. She nodded slowly. "Thanks. Now's not the time or place, but thanks for not thinking I'm crazy."

"You are one of the most rock solid women I know and definitely not crazy." The music stopped and there was a rustle of sound from the stage. "Looks like practice is over. I'll head out. See you at school tomorrow," Ginger said as she stood up from her seat.

"You got it." Janie stood, collected her papers and slipped them into her backpack before striding up to the stage to wait for Stella and her friends.

* * *

TRAVIS WALKED down the dock at Otter Cove Harbor, looking out over the bay as he made his way to his friend's boat. A bracing wind was gusting across the water, ruffling its surface and setting the boats in the harbor to rocking in the choppy waves. Otter Cove Harbor was tucked in a tiny cove off of Kachemak Bay. The cove was encircled by rocky bluffs and offered a glorious peek into the bay. He was meeting

Nathan Winters to help pull his family's boat out of the harbor for the winter. Nathan was a good friend he'd met picking up extra work years ago. A few summers of crewing with Nathan and his brothers had eventually brought him to move to Diamond Creek. Nathan and his two brothers ran a fishing charter business that catered to tourists all summer. They also had a commercial fishing vessel, which did several runs a year in between fishing charters. Travis helped out here and there for Nathan and his brothers because they offered him free charter trips in exchange, a win-win.

Travis saw Nathan wave from the boat ahead as he approached. "Hey man!" he called out once he was within earshot.

Nathan leaned against the boat railing and grinned. "Hey yourself. Damn windy out today. I thought about calling this off, but I figured I had your help, so we might as well." Nathan's dark curls blew wild in a gust of wind. He shook his hair away from his face with a laugh, his blue eyes crinkling at the corners.

Travis reached the boat and grabbed a line to tug it flush with the dock. He climbed over and glanced around to see gear spread out over the deck. "Was the plan to make a mess before I got here?"

Nathan's laugh rang out over the wind. "Nah. Just pulling everything out of the cabin. Come on, I've got bins over here."

Travis quickly got into the swing with Nathan. In short order, they had all the gear emptied from the boat. Travis used a large flat cart to roll everything to the top of the dock where Nathan's older brother Jared met them.

Jared shared Nathan's dark curls, but they were paired with sharp green eyes. He was leaning against his black truck and chatting with his wife Susie who had the passenger window rolled down when Travis reached them. When Travis first met the brothers, Jared came across as somewhat serious with an uptight edge. Over time, Travis observed the brothers play to each other's strengths in how they ran their business. Jared was definitely the detail man. Since he married Susie, Travis had seen his serious edge soften. Susie leaned out the window and grinned widely, her brown curls blowing in a swirl around her face. "Hey Travis! Nathan's making you do the hard part," she said with a wrinkle of her nose.

Travis returned her smile with a shrug as he brought the cart to a stop by the truck. "Depends. He loaded most of this, so this wasn't too bad."

Jared stepped to the back of his truck and opened it. "Let's load up."

As usual, Jared was goal oriented. Travis immediately started transferring bins from the cart to the truck. Susie jumped out and helped as well. Within a few minutes, they had the cart emptied. Susie put her hands on her hips and glanced between them, her warm brown eyes gleaming. "Great job boys! What now?"

Jared glanced over to her. "Now we go unload this stuff up at Nathan's place. I'll drop you off at the house first."

Susie eyed him for a long moment, her grin slowly fading. "You're not dropping me off. I'll help," she replied, a hint of defiance in her tone.

Jared held her gaze for a long moment. "Susie…"

Susie looked to Travis. "He's being ridiculous. I'm

pregnant again and now he wants me to sit around all the time. Could you talk some sense into him?" she asked with a huff.

Travis glanced between them. Jared shook his head slowly, resignation entering his gaze. "Susie, there's no need…"

"Oh my God!" She threw her hands up. "I'm going to lose my mind if you do this for another six months."

Travis couldn't help but grin as he watched them. He'd watched them together time and again, and had come to understand the sparring between them was how they expressed their love for each other. He caught Jared's eyes. "Not so sure how to help you here." He flicked his gaze back to Susie. "But, if you're worried they need help, that's what I'm here for. I was already planning to follow Nathan up the hill once we got the boat on the trailer."

Susie rolled her eyes. "There you go, being helpful again." She stepped to Jared's side and slipped her hand through his elbow. "Fine. I'll let Travis help, but only because he's here to help. *Not* because I'm pregnant and need to rest."

Jared dipped his head and dropped a kiss on her cheek. "Thanks babe. I'll cook dinner tonight."

Travis felt an odd pang. For a flash, he felt as if he was interrupting an intimate moment, if only because of the clear love between them. He couldn't help but wonder what it might be like if he could have that with Janie. *Dude, all you had was one dinner with her. Just where the hell do you think you're going with this?*

He gave a mental shake, his attention drawn back when Nathan called his name. He glanced over to see Nathan striding to the top of the docks, holding a set of keys aloft and jingling them. "You forgot these!" he called out.

Nathan reached them and tossed the keys to Travis. "Meet me at the boat ramp in five, okay?"

"Got it. See you in a few." Travis glanced back to Jared and Susie. "See you up at Nathan's place in a bit." At that, he jogged off.

Not much later, he was standing in the kitchen at Nathan's place. Once upon a time, Nathan shared the home with his brothers, but Luke and Jared had both gotten married. Nathan had too, but it simply worked out that he remained in the house with his wife Tess. The lower portion of the two-story timber frame home served as the office and storage for the fishing business he shared with his brothers.

"Mind if I wash my hands real quick?" Travis asked, glancing to Nathan who'd just sat down at the kitchen table with a sigh.

"Of course not!" Tess answered before Nathan had a chance. She stood by the counter, her honey-gold curls pulled up in a ponytail. "I just made some coffee for you guys anyway."

Nathan ran a hand through his hair and waved Travis toward the kitchen sink. "Wash your hands and have a seat." He glanced to Tess as she stepped to the table with two mugs of coffee in her hands. He took a hearty swallow from the mug she handed him and wrapped his arm around her waist. "Thanks for the coffee," he said with a wink.

Tess ruffled his hair and slipped away to return to the counter. After drying his hands, Travis plunked down in the chair across from Nathan where Tess had placed a mug of coffee. After a long swallow, he sighed and looked over at her where she was busy chopping vegetables. "Coffee's delicious," he said with a nod.

She glanced up, her ginger eyes warm with her smile. "Thanks. Figured you guys could use it after a few hours at the harbor. It's windy and cold out today. I bet we'll get snow tonight or tomorrow."

"Should we bet dinner?" Nathan asked with a wink.

Tess cocked her head to one side and rolled her eyes. "You already promised we'd go to dinner tomorrow night anyway. Plus, actually betting on the weather is silly."

Nathan shrugged. He tended to look for the joke in anything. He looked over at Travis. "Well, one boat's out of the water for winter. Thanks for helping us get that done."

"Glad to. Before you know it, I'll be hitching a ride on one of your charters." Travis took another sip of coffee, savoring the rich flavor and warmth. "Gotta say, I'm not much for betting on the weather myself, but I wouldn't be surprised if snow flies again tonight."

Nathan chuckled. "Well, it's November in Alaska. It's what we get."

"No complaints from me. I love snow," Travis said.

"I don't mind the snow, but driving in it stresses me out," Tess said with a pause in her chopping.

"Give it a few more years, and you'll be used to it," Nathan offered.

Tess blew an errant curl out of the way and rolled her eyes. "Hon, I've been here over four years now."

Nathan arched a brow. "Has it been that long?"

Tess threw a dishtowel at him, which Nathan deftly caught. "Kidding. It's easy to remember when you moved here because John was over one then. He just started first grade this year." Nathan caught Travis's eyes. "Damn, that makes me feel old." He was referring to his brother Luke's son. The moment he mentioned first grade, Travis thought of Janie.

Before Travis realized what he was doing, he asked a question. "First grade, huh? Is his teacher Janie Stevens?"

Tess paused in her chopping and looked over at him. "Actually, yes. Hannah was all excited he got her because everyone loves her. Not to be weird, but since when do you ask about kids' teachers?"

Nathan looked at him askance. Travis took a gulp of coffee, trying to mask his sudden discomfort. "Uh, I had to do the annual fire safety talks to the school a few weeks back. Janie was my tour guide for the day." His explanation was entirely factual, but nothing he said addressed the fact his curiosity stemmed solely from his intense fascination with Janie, a fascination he was hoping wasn't too obvious.

Tess got a gleam in her eyes and put a hand on her hip. "Speaking of betting, I'd bet money Janie's the woman you had dinner with the other night."

Travis nearly choked on his coffee. While he sputtered, Nathan snagged a napkin from the holder in the center of the table and tossed it his way. Travis wiped the coffee off his collar and looked to Tess. "What are you talking about?" he finally asked, flabbergasted that Tess knew he had dinner with anyone, much less with Janie.

"Oh geez. You know how gossip is around here. You happen to be one of the few eligible bachelors around town who also happens to be nice and handsome." She cut her eyes to Nathan who was shaking with laughter. With a shake of her head, she continued. "So, if you didn't know it, people take note when you take a woman out to dinner. I just didn't know who. By the look on your face, I'm right about Janie. Well, she's awesome, so you'd better treat her right," Tess said firmly before resuming her chopping.

Travis absorbed her comment and had to bite back the urge to ask more about Janie, wanting to know the minute details of why Tess thought Janie was awesome. He completely agreed, but it was based on nothing more than a feeling. The phone rang with Tess answering, the topic quickly derailed when she asked Nathan a question about Jared picking up supplies in Kenai. Somehow, Travis got through his coffee without any more comments about Janie. When he stood to leave, Nathan walked him to the front door and paused before opening it. "Ignore the gossip," he said with a wink.

Travis shifted his shoulders. "Usually do," he replied.

Nathan's hand was on the doorknob, but he didn't turn it. He pinned a thoughtful gaze on Travis. "You like her," he said firmly. "Good. It's about damn time."

Travis's mouth nearly fell open. "What is with you and Tess today? I took Janie to dinner. Not a big deal." Just saying her name sent a flash of longing through him as he recalled the feel of her lips under his.

Nathan chuckled. "Maybe it's not a big deal, but it sure seems like it. Anyway, Janie's awesome, so play nice."

"I always play nice," Travis countered, slightly affronted.

"Maybe so, but you're super casual. That's not

really Janie's style. Wouldn't hurt you to consider something else."

Travis stared at Nathan and finally shook his head slowly. "Since when do you care about my love life, or lack thereof?"

"Don't think about it much, but I saw the look on your face when Janie came up. I know that look because I had it once. I married the woman who made me feel like that, and it was the best decision I ever made. Just sayin'."

At that, Nathan turned the knob and waved Travis out with another grin. Travis was relieved to escape, feeling thrown by Nathan's observation. Nathan had fallen for Tess *hard* back when they first met. Travis wasn't quite sure what to think of how Nathan interpreted his reaction to Janie. He wouldn't deny she'd grabbed ahold of him, in more ways than one. Yet, thinking about a woman in terms of commitment wasn't something he did. Janie was in her own category though. He might not have thought too far ahead, but he knew the way he felt about her was more powerful than anything he'd experienced before.

CHAPTER 6

*J*anie walked gingerly down the path to her car. It had snowed again last night, leaving a fresh blanket of white fluff behind. She felt a thump against her knees, which sent her feet skidding on the icy path. She landed in a heap. "Oomph!"

A wiggly bundle of black fur encircled her in wags. "Pansy! You knocked me over!"

Stella's giggle came from behind. "Sorry! I tried to catch her, but she slipped out the door too fast."

Pansy was the six-month old puppy Stella had persuaded Janie to adopt just yesterday. Pansy wiggled madly and lapped kisses on Janie's face. Stella reached her side and held out a hand. Janie grabbed it and got back on her feet. They watched together while Pansy ran in circles through the snow. "Well, she might be house trained, but she's still a puppy," Janie said with a laugh.

Stella volunteered at the local animal shelter whenever she could, mostly walking and feeding the dogs. Pansy had suffered the fate of having her owners move away. Janie never understood how someone could decide to take an animal into their life and then just discard it like used furniture when they moved, but it happened far more than she liked to think about. The shelter was constantly overflowing with pets in need of homes. Stella had fallen in love with Pansy and pleaded with Janie to bring her home.

Janie glanced sideways at Stella whose smile stretched from ear to ear when Pansy raced back to them and circled Stella's legs. Janie's heart felt so full, it almost hurt. Joy was rare to witness in Stella. By nature, she tended toward being reserved. Any moment that pushed her to the other side was worth it. Janie looked away when snow flew up in her face as Pansy ran in a wiggling circle around her before racing away again. Stella suddenly threw her arms around Janie. "Thanks Mom!"

When Stella stepped back, her eyes were bright. "I know she'll be lots of work and she's kinda nuts, but I've never had a dog and I love her," Stella said, so earnestly, Janie's heart squeezed a little tighter.

She leaned forward and dropped a kiss on Stella's cheek. "No thanks needed. She's wild, but she's a sweetie."

Janie watched as Stella whirled away and ran through the snow to chase Pansy. A while later, Janie finished filling the dishwasher and closed it. It was Saturday morning, which was her typical morning for house chores. Stella usually helped, but Janie let her off the hook today to take Pansy over to the local dog park with a friend. As she wiped down the counter and stove, Travis meandered into her thoughts. He mostly waited in the shadows all the time now. She felt idiotic about the whole situation. It was one dinner. Nothing more. She didn't even know if he planned to call her ever again. She supposed that would have been fine, but that damn kiss made her want all kinds of things.

Despite the reinforced walls she'd built up around herself, she couldn't help the thrumming curiosity about Travis and, no matter how much she fought against it, she wanted to see him again. She wanted a chance to see if that kiss could go somewhere more. She flushed just thinking about it. With a sigh, she moved on from the kitchen to the bathroom. With her nervous energy and mental restlessness, she was cleaning like mad. At this rate, her house would be cleaner than it had been in years.

Early that afternoon, there was a loud knock at the front door. Janie stood up from the couch in the living room where she'd been idly flipping through channels and went to answer the door. Travis was standing on the other side. Her pulse lunged and her stomach tightened, but not out of desire. She didn't know how she knew, but something was wrong.

"What?"

"Stella was in a sledding accident. She…"

"Oh my God!" Janie exclaimed, cutting into what he was saying, panic flashing through her. "Is she okay? Where is she?" Janie whirled away from the door and stuffed her feet into her boots.

She started to push past Travis in the doorway when he curled his hand around her arm. "Slow down. Stella's on her way to the hospital right now. I was the last one on the scene, so when I realized it was her, I came straight here to get you. I've also got her dog in my truck. Get your coat and I'll drive you to the hospital."

With her gut clenching and fear knotting in her chest, she could hardly think. Travis's calm manner steadied her. She glanced up at him. "How do you know she's okay?"

"Because I saw her. Looks like she broke her ankle, but she should be okay. Get your coat, and I'll take you to the hospital," he said, repeating his earlier directions.

Janie's throat was tight with worry, but she was already shivering in the icy cold. His hand on her arm was a spot of warmth. She turned and stepped back through the door. He followed her through and waited while she tugged her down jacket on and snagged her purse. Moments later, she climbed into his truck. Pansy greeted her by climbing into her lap and licking her face. "Pansy! Hi sweetie," Janie said between dog kisses. "Hang on, you need to get in the back," she said once Travis joined them in the truck. With a little push, Pansy wiggled her way into the backseat of the truck, her tail whacking them in the face on the way.

"Do you mind having her in here? We could leave her in the house."

Travis had started to put his truck in gear. "I don't mind having her in here, but once we're at the hospital, it might be better if she's home."

Janie nodded quickly and glanced over her shoulder to Pansy. "Come on, Pansy. Let's go!"

Pansy bounded behind her through the snow. Janie and Stella had already done their best to dog proof the house. Pansy promptly curled up on her dog bed in the living room. Once Janie was back in the truck beside Travis, he quickly backed out of the driveway and headed toward the hospital.

"Do you know what happened?" she asked.

"Got a call some kids were sledding at the park and two of the sleds collided. Three kids were injured. I was out on another call for a moose that was hanging out a little too close to a home and charged at the neighbors. When I got to the park, Stella's ankle was stabilized, but it definitely sounds like she broke it. I didn't wait around because I wanted to get you as soon as I could."

Janie's worry didn't let up. She figured it wouldn't until she knew for certain Stella was okay. She took a slow breath and looked out the window, watching the white landscape roll by. The hospital was only a few minutes from her house. Travis rolled into the circular entrance and glanced over at her. "Go on in. I'll park and meet you inside in a few."

Janie unbuckled her seatbelt and jumped out, running quickly inside to the nurse's desk at the ER. "Hey, is..."

"Stella's already on her way into the examining room," a voice said.

Janie swung her eyes away from the woman at the computer to find Helena Clark stepping through a doorway behind the circular desk. Helena was a nurse at the hospital and an old friend of her mother's. "Can I go with her?" Janie asked, relieved to find Helena on duty today.

Helena's bright blue eyes crinkled at the corners with her smile as she nodded. "Of course you can." Helena set a clipboard on the desk and rounded its corner to hook her hand in Janie's elbow. "Come on. I just saw her. She's in some pain. We need to determine how bad the break is and set it."

Within seconds, Helena was leading her into the examining room. Stella was stretched out on the table, her face pale and her dark eyes worried. She rolled her head to the side. "Mom!"

Janie reached the table and leaned over to brush Stella's tangled hair away from her face. "Hey sweetie, how do you feel?"

Stella tried to roll her eyes, but she grimaced instead, her eyes filling with tears. "My ankle hurts. Really bad."

Janie leaned her hip against the table and curled her hand into Stella's where it was resting at her side. "I'm sorry. Helena says you're gonna be okay. Right?" Janie asked, glancing to Helena who'd stepped to the other side of the table.

Helena nodded. "You'll be fine. We'll get it set and you'll feel better soon."

Stella bit her lip and sighed. "I can't believe this. It's gonna mess up my recital practice and…"

Janie's anxiety eased now that she'd finally laid eyes on Stella and let up even more to hear Stella already starting to worry about something other than her ankle. She gave Stella's hand a squeeze. "A broken ankle won't interfere with your recital, so stop worrying about it."

Helena's pager buzzed. "I'll be back, ladies. Hold tight and the x-ray tech will be here in a few."

A while later, Janie found Travis sitting in the waiting room. Helena had shooed her out of the room when it came time to set the break. The x-ray had shown a clean break in Stella's fibula in her lower calf, along with a fracture of her patella at the knee. Travis glanced up when Janie walked in. "How is she?" he asked.

Janie plopped down in the chair beside him with a sigh. "Like you said. She's fine. I mean, she broke her ankle and fractured her knee, but she'll be fine. She's already worried about missing recital practice, so I take that as a good sign."

Travis chuckled and arched a brow. "I suppose so. I checked in with Helena, and she said they should have her ready to discharge in another hour. Do you want me to wait and bring you both home, or would you rather me take you back to your car?"

Janie met his eyes, unable to stop the thump of her heart at his concern. "Um, if you need to be somewhere…"

He shook his head quickly. "Not at all. Just asking because I didn't know what you wanted. Happy to wait and bring you both home."

She swallowed and nodded, confused by her body's almost instantaneous reaction to Travis. She'd been so focused on making sure Stella was okay earlier, she'd barely noticed him. Now that she knew Stella was going to be fine, her body swung its attention like a beam on him. His light brown hair was mussed. He was so undeniably masculine. Even sitting here in the waiting room at the hospital, a decidedly un-sexy environment, he oozed pure maleness. His chiseled features stood out in the stark fluorescent lighting. He was lounging in the chair, his muscled thighs evident under his worn denim jeans.

Her pulse skittered off and heat slid through her veins. She had to force herself to think. *For crying out loud, you're waiting for Stella at the hospital and you're sitting here getting all hot and bothered. Get a grip and now.* She gulped in air and fiddled with the zipper on her jacket before glancing back to Travis. "If you don't mind, a ride would be nice."

"Of course," he replied calmly.

She could only think he wasn't as rattled by her presence as she was by his because he managed to seem normal, while her body was going haywire all on its own.

Travis stood on one side of Stella, his hand carefully holding her by the arm. Janie stood on Stella's other side. "Stella, don't rush this. You'll need practice on your crutches, and it's probably not the best idea to try when it's icy on the path," Janie said, gesturing with her free hand to the icy walkway leading to the front porch of their home.

A messy precipitation had begun to fall while they were in the hospital, a mix of rain, sleet and snow. "Slurry" as described by Stella. As such, the path was icy and slippery, and Travis had discovered Stella had a stubborn streak. He'd barely gotten to her side in time to keep her from falling.

"Mom, I have to learn sometime," Stella protested.

Janie's eyes met his. He glanced to Stella's whose chin was set. He gave Janie a small nod. "Okay, Stella, here's the deal. You can try this, but I'm staying right by your side. The last thing you need is to fall right now."

Stella didn't look his way, but she sighed dramatically. Travis figured she'd had just enough painkillers to make her oblivious to the possible pain if she slipped and fell right now. With him on one side and Janie on the other, Stella made her way slowly and laboriously down the path. Once they got inside, Janie set Stella up on the couch with plenty of blankets and hot cocoa before looking over at Travis. "You want to stay for some dinner? I have a salmon casserole all ready to go in the oven."

Travis looked over at her. Her rich brown hair tumbled around her shoulders and her hazel eyes were bright in the soft light in the living room. Once Janie had steadied after learning Stella would be okay, his body had tuned into her. His reaction to her was off the charts. All she had to do was exist, and his body hummed with electricity and raw need. He realized he hadn't answered her question when she angled her head to the side. "Dinner would be great," he belatedly replied. He couldn't have considered any other answer.

"Great. Let me..." Her words trailed off when she looked down to see Stella sound asleep. With a soft smile, she looked up at him. "Well, I was going to see if she wanted anything, but I guess I don't have to worry about that."

She angled her head toward the kitchen before walking quietly past the couch. He followed her, sitting on a stool by the island in the middle of the kitchen when she pointed him there. "Wine or beer?" she asked as she paused by the refrigerator.

"Beer will do."

She pulled out a beer from the local brewery and slid it across the counter to him before pouring a glass of red wine for herself. Travis watched as she puttered about the kitchen, turning the oven on and transferring the casserole pan to the oven. They chatted quietly with Janie asking him questions about his work. At one point, she went to check on Stella and helped Stella make her way to bed. Janie returned a few moments later.

"She's already out. She won't dare say it out loud, but she's exhausted. I think the painkillers they gave her knocked her out," Janie said with a rueful smile.

"I'd bet she's tired. Between the adrenaline rush in the sledding accident and then the pain from the break, she should be."

Janie checked the casserole and turned back, idly twirling the oven mitt on the end of her finger. "I never did ask exactly how the sledding accident happened. Do you know?"

"I know as much as I can without having been there when it happened. Apparently, they were racing sleds down the big hill at the park. Happens almost every day in the winter, so that's no big deal. Not sure what caused it, but two sleds collided toward the bottom. Stella's leg got caught on the other sled. That flung her off her sled and into a tree. She could've broken her leg when it got caught on the other sled or when she hit the tree. Hard to know unless she remembers feeling it when it happened."

Janie grimaced when he recounted what he'd been told about the accident. With a shake of her head, she sighed. "Guess it could've been much worse. She'll be good and cranky about managing on her crutches, but she'll be fine, so I'll take it."

The oven timer beeped, interrupting their conversation. Janie turned away to check the casserole. Declaring it ready, she quickly pulled it out of the oven and served him a plate with a healthy heaping of salmon casserole, which was a delectable blend of salmon, cream cheese and cauliflower with rice. Time passed in a blink and before he knew it, Janie was putting dishes in the dishwasher, while he couldn't seem to keep his eyes off the luscious curves of her bottom.

A jolt of lust hit him, and Travis shifted in his chair. Once she'd served dinner, they'd moved over to the round table in the corner of the kitchen. He glanced out the window into the darkness. The messy snow had stopped, and the sky was clearing with stars peeking out from behind the clouds. He was wrestling with a mix of feelings. The comfort of having dinner with Janie was unusual. Her home was warm and, well, homey. Being with her through the afternoon as she'd waited to know Stella was okay and then helping them get home was a role he'd never held. As a firefighter and emergency responder, he was quite accustomed to dealing with emergencies and offering support throughout. However, his role was confined to the crisis at hand and its aftermath. Spending the afternoon with Janie this way had felt oddly comfortable. There was that and the almost constant buzz of attraction once they were alone.

She was an incredibly tempting combination of warm, nurturing and sexy as hell. Right now, she was wiping down the counter and all he could think about was how much longer he'd have to wait to feel her curves against him again. She'd demurred when he'd offered to help clean up, limiting him to carrying the dishes over to the sink and then shooing him back to the table. At that moment, she turned and leaned over to wipe down the counter facing him. His eyes dipped down to the shadowed valley between her breasts. She wore a cotton shirt with a scoop neck, which hugged her curves. He shifted in his seat again, restless from the lust pounding through his body.

She straightened, her eyes locking with his across the room. Electricity sizzled through the air between them. She spun away, snapping the moment. The sound of the water running in the sink barely penetrated when she rinsed and put the sponge away. He didn't realize what he was doing until he was on his feet, walking toward her, but he felt a sudden sense of relief when she turned and her eyes widened to find him standing beside the island a few feet away.

Her cheeks were flushed. He could see the rise and fall of her breath. He held still for only a moment before closing the distance between them. She tilted her head back to look up at him. The second her gaze collided with his, he took another step closer until he could feel the heat of her body. He didn't know what he was doing or how she felt about it, but all he knew was the drive to touch her and be close. Whatever thoughts were passing through her mind, he saw an answering desire reflected in her eyes. He lifted his hand and traced along her collarbone, up her neck where the skin was so soft it sent a pang through him, and into her silky hair. Her breath hitched, and his body tightened in response, the coil of need winding tighter inside. On the heels of a breath, he dipped his head and finally, finally brought his lips to hers.

It was like coming up for air after too long under water. He'd only kissed her once before, and he hadn't stopped craving another kiss since then. For a flash, she froze and then sighed. It was as if their interrupted kiss from the other night picked up right where it left off. He fit his mouth over hers and delved inside. She met him stroke for stroke. Somewhere along the way with their tongues tangling wildly, he found himself lifting her up onto the counter behind her. He tore his lips free from hers, frantic for a taste of her skin. Blazing a path of kisses along the column of her neck, he growled against her skin when she shifted her hips restlessly against him. Without an ounce of calculation, the subtle arch brought the heat of her core against his rock-hard cock, sending a throb of need through him.

*   *   *

JANIE COULDN'T GET CLOSE ENOUGH to Travis. With need pounding through her, she curled her legs around his hips and slipped her hands under his shirt, sighing at the feel of the muscled planes of his chest. She was lost in a maelstrom of sensation, drenched with need, and all she could think about was getting as close as possible. Meanwhile, his lips meandered along her collarbone, sending little shocks of pleasure through her everywhere they landed. His hand loosened in her hair and stroked down her back before tracing the dip of her waist and along the undersides of her breasts. She was panting with need. This wild, frantic side of herself was nearly unrecognizable to her. She didn't lose control when it came to men. Ever. But right here, right now, she was dangerously close to it and barely hanging onto the thinnest thread of control.

When he tugged her shirt down below her breasts, a moan escaped as he traced his finger around a taut nipple pressed against the navy silk of her bra. She gripped his hair when he leaned forward and laved the silk. She was slick with need, her channel throbbing. He didn't let up, alternating his attention between her nipples until she was gasping and flexing into his touch. She stroked a hand between them, curling it over the hard length of his cock. She could feel the heat of him through the denim and felt a wash of satisfaction when he groaned and lifted his head.

When his eyes met hers, dark with desire, she suddenly realized she was on the verge of tearing his clothes off right here in the kitchen. The shock of the moment sunk in. Something must've shown on her face because he held still, his eyes watching her. She forced herself to think through the haze of passion clouding her mind. No matter how much she wanted Travis—and boy did she ever—she couldn't let this happen. Not this fast and this carelessly. She tried to take a steadying breath, but that sent her breasts rising against his chest, her taut nipples brushing against his rock-hard muscles. A rush of heat washed through her—a mix of intense need and embarrassment to find herself in this position.

As she frantically tried to gather her thoughts, Travis cleared his throat. "Maybe we should slow down," he said, his words husky.

She looked up again and saw nothing but understanding in his gaze. It made her slightly uncomfortable to discover she might be that easy to read. She forced herself to take another breath and nodded jerkily. "Maybe so. I, uh… I'm not sure what this is. I don't usually…" She stopped again and tried to slow her words, realizing the tumbling babble only ratcheted up her confusion inside. "Right, maybe we should."

He stepped back, and she let her legs fall loose from where they'd been wrapped around his hips. In seconds, he'd tugged her shirt back in place. She ran a hand through her hair and shimmied her hips off the counter when he took another few steps back. For all intents and purposes, they were just two people standing in the kitchen now. If anyone walked in, they would see nothing amiss. Yet, Janie could feel the heat sliding like liquid fire through her veins and the damp silk over her nipples. That alone sent a clenching throb through her channel and she shifted her weight from one hip to the other, restless at the sensations coursing through her.

She looked over at him again and tried to marshal her thoughts. She felt silly and discombobulated. She was so out of practice with men. Well, it wasn't as if she'd ever been in practice if she was being honest. She startled herself with what she blurted out next.

"I'm not so good at this, well, whatever this is that we're doing. I don't really date. I'm a mom and a teacher and dating never really fit into that equation. If I seem a little lost, it's because I am." Her words made her flinch. They were too bare, too honest, and she hadn't quite meant to be that blunt, but the truth simply came out.

He watched her for a few beats, his gaze inscrutable. She wanted to run and hide, but she wouldn't because she didn't want to be a coward.

"Me neither," he said with a half-grin. "It's not like I haven't dated at all, but you…well, you're different. I'm not used to half-obsessing about a kiss for days. So don't go thinking you're alone in this, because you're not."

Relief washed through her, followed by wonder.

His unflinching honesty made her feel a tiny bit less mortified by her own. She felt her smile spreading across her face.

"I guess it's good we're kinda in the same boat, huh?"

He grinned, his gorgeous blue eyes crinkling at the corners. "Suppose so. For now, I should probably go. Mind if I stop by tomorrow? I could pick some coffee up from Misty Mountain Café and maybe some pastries. What does Stella like?"

Her stomach did a little somersault, and her heart warmed. That he would think of Stella first just about made her night. She forced herself to remain where she was while he slipped into his jacket. She knew if she got close again, it would be too tempting to pick up right where they'd left off.

CHAPTER 8

Travis glanced to his side at the sound of a moose pawing the ground and huffing. To his other side stood a group of elementary school students, along with two teachers, one of whom happened to be Janie. It had been a full week since she'd blown his mind with another kiss. In the time since, he could hardly stop thinking about her. Aside from the morning he brought coffee and pastries over from Misty Mountain Café, he hadn't had a chance to see her. It was disconcerting to see her just now. He'd been called up with Ben Halloran to respond to a moose and two yearlings who'd somehow gotten into the playground at Diamond Creek Elementary. This had belatedly been discovered only after the first group of kids headed out for recess.

Travis forced his mind off of Janie. Right now, they had an irate mama moose, twenty kids and two curious calves to deal with. On top of all that, snow had fallen last night and started to melt this morning under the sunshine, leaving slick patches in the shady areas of the playground. He turned to see where Ben had gone and found him in the far corner of the playground, attempting to draw the attention of the yearlings away from the kids. Unfortunately, mama moose was between everyone and the door back into the school.

The cliché of firefighters saving cats stranded in trees was turned on its head in Alaska. Travis couldn't count how many times he'd been called to deal with errant moose. Earlier this week, he and Ben helped lift a moose calf out of a hole in the ground from an abandoned and collapsed septic field. The mama moose in that scenario had proceeded to charge them once they lifted her calf to safety. If there was one thing he could claim expertise in, it was corralling ornery moose. He glanced back to the cluster of children and caught Janie's eyes. "Whatever happens, stay put for now, okay? As long as we know where you guys are, we can make sure we keep the moose away from you. It might take a few minutes, but we'll draw the calves away and mama will follow."

Janie nodded firmly. She didn't appear fazed. Given that she'd been born and raised in Alaska, Travis surmised she'd had plenty of moose encounters. The other teacher, a young woman who was probably straight out of college, looked slightly more frazzled with her eyes wide. Janie glanced from him to the other teacher before scanning her eyes over the cluster of children. "Don't worry kids. Travis and Ben handle moose all the time. We'll be fine. We just need to stay right where we are. Okay?"

Every child's head nodded, some slowly, some fast and jerky. Ben whistled loudly, which led one of the curious calves who'd been lingering by the swing set and sniffing all around it to look over in his direction. Another whistle from Ben and the calf in question started to amble in his direction near the gate. Mama moose started to turn away, her eyes locked onto her calf. At this unfortunate moment, a little boy started to dash for the door to the building. Mama moose immediately swung back in their direction and started to move toward the little boy. Travis stepped in the boy's path and latched onto his arm, stopping his run.

The little boy looked up, his brown hair falling over his forehead. A sob escaped and he tugged his arm, trying to free it from Travis's hold. "Hey buddy, hang tight. Moose don't chase unless they see something to chase. Stay right here with me."

Another sob escaped, but the boy nodded. Thankfully, the moose had stopped her movement. Ben whistled a few more times, finally drawing the attention of the other calf, which had parked itself in a corner where alder trees stretched over the fence surrounding the playground. Alder branches were a favored food of moose, so this little calf had found a handy feeding spot. Once the calf started to move and its mother's attention was firmly fixed away from the children, Travis shooed the little boy back toward Janie and started to follow slowly behind the mother moose.

He and Ben had quickly mapped out a plan when they arrived. The first order was to get the mama moose away from the gap between the children and the door. That meant drawing her away from the gate into the playground. The gate had likely been left unlocked, which made it possible for the moose to push right through in their quest of curiosity and to reach the alders. As soon as mama moose ambled far enough away, Travis turned back and waved to Janie and the other teacher, gesturing rapidly to the door. The plan was for everyone to get inside and then Travis would take Ben's place with whistles and distractions to draw the calves back to the gate. Between the two of them, they figured they could herd the calves out and mama would follow.

All was going quite well. Janie and the other teacher quietly guided the children toward the door. Until another little boy broke free from the orderly line and dashed toward Ben and the moose heading in his direction. Travis instantly recognized Danny, the little boy from Janie's classroom who had such a hard time sitting still. The look on his face was one of pure excitement. Ben moved quickly, calling out to keep the attention of the moose on him, but little Danny was a wild, tumbling blur of color as he hit an icy patch and skidded onto his bottom. Travis angled sideways to grab Danny, just as Janie came racing in his direction as well. There was simply too much happening for mama moose not to notice.

Even though everything happened in mere seconds, it felt like slow motion. Travis saw Janie racing to catch Danny and start to slip and fall. Mama moose turned away from her calves and Ben, her eyes locking onto Danny and Janie. Travis didn't even think, but spun in between the moose and Janie and Danny, dashing past them to lead her away. He heard her hooves thumping the ground behind him. Moose appeared inexplicably slow when they moved. Even when they were running, they looked as if they were ambling along. Problem was, they were tall—ranging from five feet to six and a half feet at the shoulder—

with long legs and covered a lot of ground. He heard several voices call out, but with the sound of the hooves getting closer, he aimed straight for the piece of play equipment in the center of the playground, hooking his hand on the rung of the bars and swinging himself up just as the moose reached him.

A moment later, he stood atop the bars and looked out over the playground. Ben was laughing from where he stood in the corner. The two calves had stopped to look back and were staring curiously at him. Mama moose had stopped underneath the bars and was pawing the ground, huffing and snorting. Travis glanced over to see Janie tugging Danny along at her side to the door. Danny, oblivious to any risk, was wrestling against her grip on his arm.

"But Ms. Stevens, I'm fine! I just fell on my bum. Mr. Travis is on the play set and I wanna..."

"Danny, you just about got yourself stomped by a moose! You are going right through this door..."

Her voice faded as she firmly brought Danny through the door and it shut behind her. The relief that rushed through Travis was so intense, his knees almost gave way. He hadn't been able to really think about the danger Janie and Danny were in, but he'd been flat terrified. Moose weren't predatory creatures, but they protected themselves and most certainly protected their calves. A few strikes of hooves from a moose had the potential to kill, even if that wasn't what the moose set out to do. He gave himself a mental shake and glanced down. Mama moose had stopped pawing the ground and was looking up at him. He could almost reach out and touch her ears, which were rotating so wildly as she listened in all directions that it was almost comical.

He glanced across the playground to Ben. "So much for that plan," he called out.

Ben's laughter carried across the playground with a gust of icy wind blasting behind it. Travis took stock and realized he was in a precarious position and useless to Ben where he was. The door to the school building opened again, and Janie stepped through. She stayed right where she was and gave a wave. "How about I make some noise over here to draw the calves this way?" she called, her voice lilting over the wind.

"Perfect!" Ben replied before Travis had a chance to discourage her plan.

He wasn't normally one to pull the whole manly routine, but he most definitely did *not* want to stand by and watch while she put herself at risk. He started to move and realized he was in no position to climb down unless he was plain stupid. Mama moose was still a mere foot away from where he stood above her. Janie, being the true blue Alaskan she was, didn't bother to wait for his reply. Once Ben shouted his agreement with her idea, she started whistling, clapping and stomping her feet.

With his gut clenching, Travis had to physically hold back from climbing down as he watched Janie run alongside the building until she reached the playground gate where she banged on the aluminum bars. The calves finally began to move in her direction. With one last baleful look at Travis, mama moose ambled away. With Ben bringing up the rear, Travis climbed down and dashed to Janie.

Moments later, mama moose was walking through the gate after a nip on the haunches of one of her calves who was lingering by the alder. She seemed to have decided the snacking wasn't worth the noise and commotion. Ben was closing the gate when Travis reached Janie. Without thinking, he pulled her into his arms, another intense wave of relief rocking him. He leaned back and looked down into her face. Her cheeks were rosy from the cold and her eyes bright, the layers of green and gold mesmerizing.

She stared up at him, her lips parting. Need raced through him, yet he knew now wasn't the time or place, especially not when her eyes shifted from startled to snappy. "Good grief! Were you worried I was going to get hurt?"

She took a step back. She eyed him for a long moment. "You almost got run down by the moose on purpose and you were worried about me?" She put her hands on her hips and rolled her eyes. "I'm not stupid. Once I got Danny out of the way, I figured maybe you guys could use a little extra distraction since you were trapped on top of that." She gestured dismissively to the play set in question, glancing to Ben when he approached them.

Ben's brown eyes gleamed as he glanced between Travis and Janie. He didn't comment, but looked to Janie. "Thanks for the assist. Once Trav got stuck, well, we coulda worked it out, but you were a big help."

Janie's smile stretched across her face. "No problem." Her eyes flicked between them. Travis wasn't embarrassed about ending up trapped. He hadn't had any other options at the moment, but he got Janie's message loud and clear. She was accustomed to taking care of herself and didn't take kindly to anyone else stepping in the path.

He forced himself to beat back the need to wrap

her in his arms again. A few risky moments had sent him stumbling inside. She stood before him, practically glowing with vitality in the cold, winter afternoon. He gulped in the bracing air and cast his eyes between her and Ben. "You know I only ended up there trying to get the moose's attention off of Danny. Boy, he's a handful, huh?"

Janie grinned. "I keep telling him if we could only figure out how to channel his energy." Her grin faded. "Seriously, thanks for that. He moves like lightning and broke free from the line before I even realized it. Anyway, I need to get back to class. I'll catch you guys later, okay?"

"You got it," Ben said as he spun around and headed toward their vehicle.

Travis watched Ben walk away, surprised at his rapid retreat. He glanced down at Janie, thoughts tumbling through his mind. Mostly, he just wanted to ask her if he could see her again. Now would be his preference, but that wasn't an option. "Don't suppose I could bring dinner over?" he asked abruptly. He figured with Stella hobbling about on crutches and it being a school night, dinner out and about wasn't an option.

Janie stared up at him, her hazel eyes pulling at him. She finally nodded, her cheeks flushing a deeper shade of pink. "Sure."

Her one word answer pleased him so much, a grin split his face. "What's Stella's favorite takeout?"

"Glacier Pizza. She'd eat it all day, every day if I let her."

"Done."

Moments later, he caught up to Ben and climbed

into the truck beside him. "Ready?" he asked once the engine rumbled.

Ben glanced to him. "Of course."

Travis started driving back to the station. He was pulling into the parking lot when Ben spoke again. "So, Janie Stevens, huh?"

Travis brought the truck to a stop and glanced to Ben. "What about Janie?" he asked.

Ben threw his head back with a laugh. "Dude, you're worse off than I thought." He unbuckled his seat belt and started to climb out. "By the way, Janie's awesome." He threw that comment over his shoulder and strolled into the building, leaving Travis to wonder just how ridiculously obvious he was.

CHAPTER 9

"Mom!" Stella called from the couch.

Janie stepped away from the sink where she'd been cleaning up the dishes left by Stella earlier today. She cornered the bottom of the staircase and glanced to Stella. "Yes?"

Stella pointed to her backpack, which was leaning against the edge of the coffee table and out of her reach. "I forgot to get my biology book out."

Janie quickly strode to the backpack and set it on the floor where Stella could reach it. Pansy had snuggled into a spot between Stella and the back of the couch. Her tail thumped against the couch when Janie came close. Janie reached over to stroke her head quickly before stepping away. For the most part, Stella had learned to navigate with her crutches, but she was constantly forgetting things like this. Janie had decided it was easier to drive Stella to school than worry about her navigating up the driveway with the winter weather settling in, which Stella just loved.

Janie glanced to Stella who'd already reached in and pulled out her massive biology tome. "So, recital practice tomorrow, right?"

Stella looked up with a nod. "Uh huh."

"How about you do your homework in Mrs. Cooper's classroom before recital? I won't have time to get over there to pick you up and bring you home in between."

Stella shrugged. "Sure. Mrs. Cooper won't mind."

Mrs. Cooper was Stella's music teacher and her absolute favorite teacher. Mrs. Cooper took Stella under her wing early on after Stella came to live with Janie. At the time, Stella's aptitude for being surly and quiet could've won her an award had there been such a thing. Mrs. Cooper saw through it and supported Stella's natural ability at piano, a much healthier aptitude than her surliness.

"What's for dinner?" Stella asked as she filled out an answer on her homework.

"Travis is bringing pizza. I'm supposed to text him what kind you want."

Janie's stomach did a little flip when she spoke his name aloud. The effect Travis was having on her was starting to make her feel half-crazy. Although she was still a little annoyed with his manly attitude at the playground today. She was perfectly capable of handling herself with moose. Anyone born and raised in Alaska had encountered them hundreds of times. Her mind wandered to his piercing blue gaze and rugged, muscled body, which sent a wash of heat through her.

"Glacier Pizza? On a school night?" Stella's questions came out rapid fire as a grin spread across her face.

"He offered, so I told him Glacier Pizza was your favorite." She glanced at the clock on the wall above the windows. "What kind do you want tonight?"

Stella wiggled gleefully on the couch, her bright pink cast rolling back and forth with her feet. "Pepperoni and…" She paused, tapping her fingertips on her book. "…one with olives and feta."

Janie couldn't help but grin. "I'll see if he's planning to get one or two pizzas."

She slipped her phone out of her pocket and texted him quickly. "I'll finish up in the kitchen while you get your homework done," she said as she turned away. Before she made it back to the sink, Travis's return text buzzed. *Two pizzas it is. See you in a bit.*

A simple reply and it sent her pulse skyrocketing. She couldn't believe she was this worked up about him bringing pizza over. She'd be having dinner with him and her teenage daughter who was laid up with a broken ankle. All in all, it was completely unromantic, yet here she was thinking about their kiss the other night. She'd barely been able to sleep after that. With her mind spinning over thoughts of Travis and her body aflame, she'd been stirred up and restless. With a forceful shake of her head, she set her phone on the counter and finished washing dishes.

A while later, Janie looked across the table at Travis. Stella had gone to bed a few minutes ago, although she'd valiantly fought against her tiredness. Janie had just returned from making sure Stella was settled in bed comfortably. She felt she might be over-worrying, but she didn't want Stella's crutches falling with a crash like they had last night. Stella was alternately annoyed with Janie's extra attention and good-natured about it. Pansy had taken to sleeping on the floor by Stella's bed as well, so Janie took comfort in thinking perhaps Pansy was worried too.

"Stella seems like she's doing okay," Travis said.

Janie laughed softly. "Most of the time. Mornings are the hardest because she likes to sleep until the absolute last minute. Being on crutches slows things down a bit, so I've been making sure she's up a good half hour early. Otherwise, she's adjusted. We didn't plan it this way, but getting Pansy when we did worked out great. She's a good distraction for Stella right now."

Travis chuckled, the low timbre of his laugh sending a prickle up her spine. "Good timing, huh? How long does she need to wear her cast?"

"They said four to six weeks. Stella *loved* hearing that." Janie shook her head. "I guess they'll take a look at four weeks and make a decision. They said she should heal pretty quickly as long as she's good about keeping it stabilized. I'm hoping for four weeks. That means she'll have it off before Christmas. If not, she'll manage."

Travis flashed a grin. "I'm sure she will. She's being a pretty good sport about it."

"After the first day, she's handled it like a champ. I'm so relieved her thing is music instead of a sport. Otherwise, who knows how many practices she'd miss? Her music teacher set up a footrest for her when she plays piano, so she's good to go."

While their conversation was focused on Stella and rather mundane, Janie's body was humming with a low current of electricity rolling through her. Her hyperawareness of him was unsettling. Restless, she stood up from the table, carrying her empty wineglass to the sink. She resisted the temptation to fill it again because she'd already had enough wine to push her close to being tipsy. She also needed to somehow keep her wits about her since she barely seemed able to do that with Travis anywhere nearby.

A prickle raced up her spine, and she spun around to find him walking across the kitchen to her, carrying an empty pizza box and his plate. When she saw him glance around as if looking for the trash, she pointed to the corner, which was conveniently far away from her. With flutters twirling in her belly, she turned back to the sink and needlessly rinsed her wineglass before putting it in the dishwasher. In seconds, he tossed the pizza box in the trashcan and walked toward the sink, setting his plate on the counter beside her.

"Can I help with clean up?"

His low voice sent another prickle up her spine and a swirl of heat in her belly. She forced herself to take a deep breath, feeling ridiculous about how at mercy she was to his presence. She turned the faucet off and angled sideways, carefully keeping a small distance between them, although every fiber of her yearned to close the distance and feel the hard muscled planes of his body against hers again. His elbow was resting on the counter, his posture relaxed and just oozing masculinity. For crying out loud, all he was doing was leaning against the counter and she could hardly keep her eyes off of him.

She looked down at the floor, but her eyes had their own ideas and immediately flicked to him again, tracking up his body. He wore faded jeans of denim so soft, his muscled legs were easily visible. With one hand hooked in a pocket, the waistband of his jeans angled down, offering a glimpse of his muscled abs. He wore a faded navy t-shirt that didn't do much to hide the planes of his chest. She doubted he worked out because she knew the life he lived kept him fit, but holy hell the man's body looked like it was carved from stone. Her eyes finally collided with his. Her pulse lunged and her breath caught. His eyes had darkened and held hers locked to his.

They stood there, frozen in place for several seconds, before Travis moved. He slowly pushed off the counter and took one step, just one step, and he was right in front of her. He cleared his throat and angled his head to the side.

"I want to kiss you," he said, his words plain and his voice gruff.

Conflicted as she was about him when she was able to think clearly, she was entirely incapable of thinking just now. All she wanted was to kiss him. *Now.*

She tried to speak, but she couldn't seem to make a sound. Wordlessly, she nodded. In a flash, he closed the fraction of distance between them and tangled his hand in her hair, fitting his mouth over hers. This kiss didn't start slow—it was a wild dive. She couldn't imagine any man kissing more masterfully than him. He kissed with pure confidence—licks, kisses and nibbles alternating with deep strokes of his tongue. By the time he pulled back, she was startled to discover she hadn't collapsed. She was aflame inside and out, her skin hot and flushed.

He lifted his head, his eyes locking with hers. The depth of need she saw there grabbed at her viscerally —an emotional, physical pull so intense she couldn't look away. They stood still, their breath heaving in the quiet kitchen. Her nipples were so tight they ached, and she could feel the moisture between her thighs. She was snapped out of her fevered state when Pansy came trotting into the kitchen, whining softly.

Janie took a quick step back with Travis straightening and turning to look toward Pansy. Still slightly unfocused with her body humming and need sliding through her, Janie glanced down at Pansy who came to her side, wagging her tail and glancing back and forth between Janie and the stairs. Janie looked over at Travis. "Let me go check on Stella. Maybe it's weird to think Pansy's trying to tell me something, but…"

He nodded. "I was thinking the same thing. Go ahead."

Janie jogged up the stairs with Pansy right on her heels and glanced in Stella's bedroom. Stella was still asleep, but she'd twisted in her sleep in such a way that her casted leg was caught at an odd angle between her bed and the wall. Janie glanced down at Pansy and stroked her head quickly. As she approached Stella's bed, she heard a soft sound from Stella. While she might be asleep, she must be in some pain. Janie carefully leaned across the bed and adjusted Stella's leg. She managed not to wake Stella and placed an extra pillow between Stella's leg and the wall to keep her from rolling like that again.

Pansy curled up with a sigh on the floor once Janie gave her another pat and walked quietly out. When she got back downstairs, Travis was leaning against the counter. "Everything okay?" he asked.

"Yeah. Her bed's right up against the wall, and her leg got twisted. She wasn't even awake, but Pansy seemed to know she wasn't comfortable." Janie shrugged. "She's a sweet dog. Anyway, I straightened it out and made sure she has a pillow by her leg. Should be fine now."

He nodded slowly, his eyes on her. Already, that hum of desire was swirling around them again. Yet, she couldn't relax. She glanced over at him, trying to figure out what to say. He saved her from bumbling through she didn't know what. He pushed back from the counter. "I should probably get going." He moved toward the kitchen door, snagging his lightweight down jacket off the coatrack. As he shrugged his jacket over his shoulders, he caught her eyes. "Look, uh…" He paused and gave his head a small shake. "I, uh, don't want you to think… Well, I don't know what you might think. I guess I was trying to say I'd like a chance to see you again."

Before she realized what she was doing, she was nodding. A slow smile spread across his face. He stepped to her and dipped his head. In seconds, she was on fire again. It seemed they weren't capable of anything like a quick, casual kiss. Travis tore his lips away from hers, swearing softly. When he glanced over at her, she couldn't keep a giggle from escaping. It was ridiculous really. He grinned. "I'd better go. How about I give you a call before the weekend?"

"Sounds good."

He held her gaze for a long moment before turning and stepping out into the cold. A blast of air came through the door when he opened and closed it. The icy air was a balm to the heat coursing through her. She shivered at the contrast. Turning away from the door, she walked to the windows at the back of the house and looked outside. Moonlight fell across the bay in a glittering path, the water rippling under its glow. The mountains were dark, hulking shapes in the night sky. Her breath gradually slowed, her pulse following. She finally made her way upstairs, poking her head around Stella's door to find her sound asleep. Pansy's tail thumped softly against the floor.

CHAPTER 10

*T*ravis kicked the door shut behind him and strode down the hall at the fire station. Winter was setting in swiftly, and it was damn freezing this morning. He headed straight for the break room. "Oh yes, fresh coffee," he commented to himself when he smelled the strong brew as soon as he stepped into the room.

"Perfect timing," a voice said.

Travis glanced up to find Darren Thomas, Diamond Creek's police chief, coming into the break room from the opposite side. The fire station and police station shared administrative support and the break room. "Hey Darren, looks like your timing's about as good as mine. You go first," he said, gesturing to the full coffee pot.

Darren flashed a smile, his brown eyes crinkling at the corners. "No argument from me." He stepped to the coffee pot, snagged a cup and filled it quickly. He passed it to Travis before filling another for himself.

"You didn't have to do that," Travis said with a laugh.

Darren shrugged. "It's a few seconds wait." He paused and took a long swallow of coffee. "Damn, I needed that." He looked to Travis. "So what's up?"

Travis had just taken his own gulp of coffee. He slowly sank down into a chair by the round table in the room. "Not much. You?"

Darren sat down across from him and brushed his brown hair out of his eyes. "The usual. With summer over, things are a little quieter for us."

Travis nodded. "You know the deal, same for us. How's Risa doing?" Risa was Darren's wife, and they were expecting their first child in a few months.

Darren, usually a somewhat somber guy, flashed a wide smile. "She's great. She keeps complaining that she feels huge, but she looks beautiful."

Travis grinned. "Well, she is beautiful. Still haven't figured out what she sees in you, but..." He let his words trail off.

Darren chuckled. "I still haven't figured out what she sees in me, but I'm not complaining." He paused to take another sip of coffee and leaned back in his chair just as Sylvia rounded the corner of the door and walked into the room.

Her eyes bounced from Darren to Travis. "Hey boys, how's it going?"

Travis lifted his cup in a greeting. "Now that I've had some of your coffee, my morning's much better."

"Ditto," Darren offered with a grin.

Sylvia stepped to the coffee pot to help herself before joining them at the table. They chatted casually for a few minutes until Ben passed by the door with a quick wave. Sylvia's gaze swung to Travis, her eyes narrowing. "What's this I hear about you and Janie Stevens?"

"Huh?" Travis asked, slightly startled at the abrupt shift in topic.

Darren pushed his chair back, the legs scraping on the floor. "Have mercy on him, Sylvia," he said with a quick grin before he clapped Travis on the shoulder on his way past the table.

Travis felt suddenly uncomfortable and shifted his shoulders before taking a slow sip of coffee. Sylvia looked at him thoughtfully. After several beats, she spoke again. "I was just teasing, you know? Ben seems to think you might have a thing for Janie. He's ready to place bets on how long it'll be before you admit it."

Travis groaned and ran a hand through his hair before leaning back in his chair. "Ben's being ridiculous."

Sylvia laughed softly. "Ben was the class clown when he was a little boy, and he hasn't changed much since then." Her expression sobered. "Based on your reaction, I'm guessing he's right about Janie."

Of all the reasons Travis hadn't gotten serious about dating, he hadn't considered the benefits of avoiding the rumor mill in Diamond Creek. Yet, even when Sylvia was teasing, she didn't tend to spread gossip. Oh, she had plenty to share if she chose. People told her just about everything. She was the human switchboard in Diamond Creek, a benevolent switchboard with everyone's best interests at heart. He took a deep breath and looked over at her.

"Ben might be right," he finally said with a sheepish shrug.

Sylvia's smile spread slowly. "Well, it's about damn

time." She paused and cocked her head to the side. "How did this come about?"

"Me and Janie?"

At her nod, he shrugged, uncertainty rolling through him. His feelings for Janie were unfamiliar and new. "After I fished her out of the bay, she ended up being my assigned tour guide the day I went to the elementary school for the fire safety talks. I asked her out to dinner and..." He shrugged again. "Honestly, not much has happened. I've had dinner with her and Stella since then, but that's about it. I'm not, well, I'm not much for dating, much less a single mother. Any suggestions?"

Sylvia took a sip of coffee. She was quiet long enough, Travis started to wonder. When she spoke, her eyes were serious. "Janie is an amazing woman, but you might want to know something about her. I'm not sure I should say anything, but if you don't hear it from me, you might hear it from someone else."

Travis's gut clenched and he took a gulp of coffee before nodding.

"Janie hasn't dated much. I kind of figured she might not ever bother with it, which tore me up. Her father died in a fishing accident when she was ten. After that, her mother got involved with Randy Price. There's no other way to say it, but Randy was a class-A abusive jerk. He knocked her mother around and pretty much isolated her from everyone. If you know much about Janie's family, that was awful. They're pretty tight. Everyone was worried, but nothing seemed to nudge her away from Randy. Anyway, one day when Janie talked back, Randy hauled off and hit her. He broke her jaw. That woke Janie's mom up, and she knocked him out with a pan. Janie ended up being the one to call the police. After that, they were back and forth in court. Randy tried to move back in with Janie's mom more than once, but she kept him away. He was eventually convicted, but he didn't spend much time in jail. I check on him every so often. He moved to Fairbanks and he's been arrested a few more times for assault against his latest girlfriend."

Sylvia stopped talking and watched him. Travis was wrestling with a mix of emotions—raw fury at a man he'd never even laid eyes on, anguish for what Janie went through watching her mother get beaten, getting assaulted herself, and then slogging through the long legal process of a trial. If he'd wondered if Janie was starting to mean something to him, he knew it with certainty now. All he wanted was to track down Randy Price and beat the living crap out of him.

"I thought maybe you'd want to know that bit of her background. She, uh, well, she's steered clear of men for the most part, and it's no wonder. I'm friends with her mother Leslie. She's never stopped feeling bad about letting Randy into their lives and not being able to push him out until he hurt Janie."

Travis managed to nod. He'd sensed how guarded Janie was and now he knew where it came from. He took a breath and another gulp of coffee, trying to beat back the fury flooding through him. Randy Price was nowhere near, and it wouldn't do much good for Travis to stomp around looking for a fight with someone long gone.

Sylvia reached across the table and curled her hand over his, giving it a squeeze. "You can't change the past, and Randy can't touch Janie now. But if I was curious about whether she meant anything to you, I'm not now." Her eyes crinkled with her smile. "Janie's stronger for what she went through, but she doesn't make it easy for anyone new to come into her life. You can count yourself lucky in that regard."

Sylvia stood up and rounded the circular table to lean over and squeeze Travis's shoulders. "Like I said, you're a good man. I have a feeling about you and Janie."

At that moment, Ben entered the break room, a wide grin spreading when he caught Sylvia's words. "Told ya!"

His teasing snapped the somber moment, which Travis needed. He shifted in his chair to glance over his shoulder. "You just wait 'til we're making bets on your love life."

Ben shrugged. "Go right ahead. I can take it," he said with a chuckle as he poured himself a cup of coffee. He stepped to Sylvia's side and dropped a kiss on her weathered cheek. "Thanks for the amazing coffee."

As Ben turned away, their radios went off simultaneously, announcing a stove fire on the hillside. Travis stood swiftly and followed Ben out. In minutes, they were racing behind the main fire truck up the hillside.

* * *

JANIE CARRIED a tray into the living room, pausing beside the coffee table to clear a spot for it. Once she set it down, she put her hands on her hips and glanced down at Stella. "Need anything else before I run upstairs to shower?"

Stella looked up from her tablet reader and

glanced to the tray. "Chocolate chip pancakes! Yay!" She lifted her eyes to Janie. "Thanks Mom. This broken ankle isn't turning out so bad," she said with a grin.

Janie rolled her eyes. "You get breakfast every Saturday. Only difference is now I carry it to you."

Stella leaned over and transferred the tray from the coffee table to her lap. Pansy wiggled her way between the couch and coffee table, nosing her head onto the edge of Stella's tray. Stella stroked her head quickly and nudged her away. "Sorry Pansy, no pancakes for you."

Janie smiled softly watching them. Pansy had blended seamlessly into their lives. It felt like she'd been there much longer. She was Stella's shadow most of the time.

"So you're all set?" Janie asked.

Stella was already chewing on a bite of pancake. She nodded and mumbled her reply between bites. "All set."

Janie jogged up the stairs and into her bedroom. After a quick shower, she returned downstairs to find her mother had pulled up a chair on the opposite side of the coffee table from Stella. Her mother stopped by frequently, so it wasn't a complete surprise. They were engrossed in a game of Scrabble, which had become one of Stella's favorite games.

Janie's mother, Leslie, glanced up. "Hey hon, thought I'd stop by and check on you two. I brought coffee from Misty Mountain." She gestured across the room to the kitchen counter.

Janie made a beeline to the counter and lifted a cup from the holder. "Thanks Mom!" She took a gulp of the rich brew and sighed. "So good." She crossed back into the living room and sat carefully on the couch by Stella's feet. She noticed Stella's tray had been carted away and guessed her mom had taken care of it.

Stella quickly played a word and lifted a fist in triumph. "Seven letter word and fifty extra points! Oh, and I'm out of letters."

Leslie grinned and gathered the tiles from the board before dumping them in the bag. "Remind me when your first recital is."

"In three weeks. After Thanksgiving and before Christmas. I hope I don't still have this thing on," she paused to point to her bright pink cast. "But, it'll be fun. You're coming, right?" It didn't matter that Janie's mother had never missed a single concert of Stella's, Stella always asked.

Leslie looked up as she put away the game board. "Of course! As if I'd ever miss one of your concerts." Her hazel eyes were warm as she looked over at Stella.

Janie had inherited her dark brown hair and hazel eyes from her mother. Leslie's hair was streaked with gray now, but her eyes were lively and snapping. Janie never stopped feeling relieved to see the joy in her mother again. It had taken a few years after Randy was successfully banished from their lives before her mother seemed to return to the woman she'd been before. Thinking about Randy made her mind skip tracks to Travis. Not because Travis was anything like Randy, but because no matter how good it felt to be with Travis, she always carried seeds of doubt about her judgment deep inside. She knew perfectly well how easy it was to be fooled. Randy hadn't walked into her mother's life and started knocking her around. It had been a gradual process of erosion in his behavior. He'd started out charming and ended up nearly destroying their lives. Janie still wondered if her mother ever would have gathered the courage to leave him if he hadn't hurt her.

Travis is nothing like him. Nothing. Don't even go there. She gave herself a mental shake. It was hard not to constantly doubt. After what she'd witnessed her mother go through, it didn't seem worth the trouble to suss out who could be trusted. Instead, she built a life where she didn't have to worry about being vulnerable.

"Mom?" Stella's question broke through her thoughts.

She glanced to Stella. "Yeah?"

"I need to shower. Can you help me get up?"

Janie stood and held her hand out. She gave a gentle pull as Stella rose up. Once Stella was standing, Janie handed her crutches over. Stella gave a little wave and made her way to the stairs. Janie had to forcibly keep herself from following Stella to the stairs. Stella had gotten more and more nimble at making her way around with her crutches and resisted any help. Janie watched while she slowly navigated up the stairs. After she disappeared down the hall, Janie tidied the pillows on the couch and folded the throw blanket before sitting down.

Her mother smiled softly. "I bet you want to hold her hand through this whole thing."

"Oh yeah. She won't let me though, so I have to suck it up."

"She's doing great. I'm glad it's not holding her back much."

"Not at all. Once we got through the first few days and her pain eased, she's been fine. She has her cranky moments, but she has those with or without a broken ankle."

"That she does. I was thinking of taking her up to Anchorage with me for today and tomorrow. Is that okay?"

"Sure. You doing your usual holiday shopping run?"

"Of course. I need to beat the Thanksgiving rush. I booked a two-room suite, so she'll have her own space. It's still early, so I figure we have plenty of time to make the drive. Need anything?"

"Always. Hang on. I'll write a list." Janie strode to the refrigerator and tore a piece of paper off a small notebook mounted there. She quickly jotted down a list of groceries and a few gift items. After she handed the list over, she crossed her legs and leaned into the pillows. "Anything new?"

Leslie shook her head. "Nope. At sixty-five, a boring life works great for me."

Janie rolled her eyes. "Mom, your life's not boring. You volunteer for the hospital and the animal shelter, and you're friends with the entire town. You have a much more exciting social life than I do." Travis flashed through her mind again, but she batted him away.

Leslie grinned. "Maybe not. Rumor has it you're seeing Travis Wilkes."

Janie felt the blush race up her neck and face. "Seriously? Where did you hear that?"

"From Stella, so it's not exactly gossip," Leslie said pointedly. "Stella thinks he's awesome."

Janie grabbed her coffee for a big gulp and sagged into the cushions. Talking about Travis made her feel unsettled because she didn't know what to do with her feelings. "I should've guessed."

"Not that you need to hear it from me, but I'm glad you're seeing someone. Travis seems like a nice guy too."

Janie closed her eyes and took a breath. "He is a nice guy. I don't know if it's gonna go anywhere. I hope Stella's not pinning her hopes on something big. It's been a few dinners and that's it." She uncrossed and crossed her legs, restless at the emotions Travis stirred up inside. She looked over at her mother. "I don't mean to bring up a bad subject, but I have to ask. Randy was nice at first, right? That wasn't just my imagination, was it?"

Her mother closed her eyes for a long moment before opening them again. They held sadness and pain. "Of course, he was nice at first. But pretty early on, I knew he wasn't who he seemed. I just didn't know how to end things and by then, things started to go really bad. Honey, don't let what happened with Randy make you question your own judgment. Travis is nothing like Randy. Nothing! You know that. Plenty of people in Diamond Creek know him and know him well." Her mother angled her head to the side. "You have no idea how much I wish I'd had the strength to leave Randy once I started to get a sense of who he was. If I could have a chance to go back and change things, I would. I can't, so all I can do is learn from it and go forward. I hope you don't think the only lesson in it was not to trust any man."

Janie's throat was tight. She held her mother's eyes and tried to keep from crying, but a tear rolled down her cheek anyway. She gave her head a sharp shake. "I don't know why all this is coming up right now. It's been so long. I thought…I guess I thought I was fine. This whole thing with Travis makes me feel like I'm not sure of anything."

Her mother leaned forward, pinning her gaze on Janie. "You don't doubt your judgment in any other part of your life, so don't do it here. Give yourself a chance for once."

Janie swallowed and took a deep breath. "Right. It just seems a lot easier not to worry about trying to find someone."

Her mother shook her head slowly. "It's one thing if you choose to be alone because that's what you want. It's another if the choice is a default option driven by fear. Your father was nothing like Randy. After he died, I was devastated and emotionally out of whack. If I'd been a little more together inside, I'd have seen Randy for who he was before he got too close. You have no idea how much I regret I didn't have the strength to leave him before he hurt you, but I didn't. I can't fix that, but I'll tell you over and over again that you deserve to have more if that's what you want. The way you looked when I mentioned Travis tells me you probably do want a chance to at least see what might unfold. Don't let fear take that away from you. That's all I'm saying."

Janie stared at her mother for a long moment and finally looked away, weary of the emotional confusion swirling inside. *See, this is why it's easier to just be alone. Yeah, but maybe I want to try something else.* She looked out over the bay. Clouds were scudding across the sky with the wind ruffling the surface of the water. She looked back at her mother and shrugged. "I'm working on it. I…" She stopped when she heard the distinctive thump of Stella's crutches on the hallway upstairs. "Let this go for now. Hang on, let me tell Stella you want to take her to Anchorage." She stood and strode to the bottom of the stairs. "Gram wants to take you to Anchorage for the night. Wanna go?" she asked as Stella reached the top of the stairs and looked down.

Stella grinned and waved one of her crutches. "Yes! When are we leaving?"

Janie's mother had joined her at the base of the stairs. "Whenever you're ready," Leslie said. "It's just for the night, so you don't need to pack much."

Stella spun around and immediately crutched her way back down the hall. "Hang on. I'll get my stuff now. Mom, can you help me carry a bag down?"

Not much later, Janie stood by the kitchen door and watched her mother's small truck disappear as it turned onto the road. They'd decided to take Pansy with them since the hotel allowed dogs. When Janie closed the door and walked through the kitchen, the house felt strangely quiet without Stella and Pansy. She started a load of laundry and puttered around the house, taking care of chores, until she ran out of things to do. Restless, she found herself pacing aimlessly back and forth in front of the windows, thoughts of Travis tumbling through her mind.

She was wrestling with figuring out how to shove him out of her mind, but didn't know if it would be that easy. She was too drawn to him and disconcertingly drawn to the humming attraction between them. She wondered if she simply needed to get him out of her system. Abruptly, she spun away from the windows. She had the rest of the day and night to herself. It would be the perfect time to see if she could do precisely that.

Travis stared down at the text message on his phone screen for roughly the one-hundredth time. He wasn't usually an indecisive man, but then he wasn't usually tossed asunder inside by a woman like Janie. He didn't know what it was about her, but just thinking about her sent him spinning inside, not to mention kept his body on high idle. He tried to recall the last time mere thoughts of a woman got him hard, and he kept coming up empty. He considered himself practical and in control. Janie made him feel wildly impractical and bordering on out of control. For instance, she'd sent him a text message a bit ago, the message he couldn't stop re-reading.

Have the house to myself until tomorrow.

That's it. That's all it said. The ball was in his court, but he didn't want to make assumptions. All he could think was that meant he could go over and finally slake the pounding lust inside. He nearly jumped when there was a knock on his truck window.

He glanced up to find Nathan grinning at him through the frosty glass. He glanced at the dashboard clock and realized he'd likely been sitting in his truck in the post office parking lot for a good five minutes. That's how much a text from Janie got to him. He gave himself a mental shake and climbed out of the truck. Nathan stepped back as Travis opened the door.

"Hey man, what's up?" Nathan asked casually.

Travis shrugged. "Not much. Just checking the mail."

He started to walk toward the post office. Nathan turned at his side and walked with him. A bracing wind gusted across the parking lot.

"Damn it's cold," Nathan commented.

They reached the door, and Travis experienced a sense of relief when the door whooshed shut behind them and the warmth inside the building rushed around him. He glanced to Nathan. "That it is. What're you up to?"

Nathan arched a brow. "Uh, same as you. Checking the mail."

They walked in tandem down one of the aisles, each respectively opening their post office boxes and pulling mail out. In silence, they stopped at a small table by the windows and sorted their mail. Travis tossed junk mail in the recycling with Nathan following suit. He glanced up and almost jumped in his skin when he saw Janie walking across the parking lot. Her dark hair blew in a swirl with a gust of wind.

"Aha. Now I know why you're so distracted," Nathan commented.

Travis looked to his side. "Huh?"

Nathan cocked his head to one side and shook his

head slowly. "You're all out of it. Janie walks across the parking lot and you can't stop staring at her. Do yourself a favor and actually do something about it."

Travis was relieved he wasn't one to blush, not because it wasn't exactly a masculine thing to do, but because it would cue Nathan to the fact he was right on target. He forced himself to take a slow breath and studiously kept his eyes off the door when he heard it open. Despite his best efforts, his eyes flicked sideways all on their own to see Janie turn the other direction toward the counter. At Nathan's low chuckle, he looked back in his direction. With a mental sigh, he shrugged. "Fine. You got me." He looked down at his mail and realized he was about to toss a bill in the recycling. "I'm a little lost here, any suggestions?"

Nathan flashed a grin. "I just told you. Do something about it. I'm no expert, but I can guess you're tiptoeing around this thing. Having been a guy who was totally clueless to finding a woman who meant a hell of a lot to me, I get it. One foot in front of the other. Take her to dinner again. Pretty sure you can handle that."

Travis absorbed Nathan's words and nodded slowly. Right. He could handle taking her to dinner. He tapped the small stack of mail left on the counter and straightened his shoulders. "I can do dinner."

Nathan's shoulders started to shake as he looked at Travis. Travis rolled his eyes. "Dude, give me a break. You were ridiculous about Tess, so don't go acting like you don't know what it's like."

Nathan gulped in air between bursts of laughter. "Fair enough. Can't help it though. You've always been calm and cool about women. It's funny to see you all tied up." He paused and glanced toward the post office counter where Janie stood in line. "I'm outta here. I'd suggest you make sure to talk to her before you leave. Keep me posted."

At that, Nathan turned and ambled out of the post office. Travis remained by the table facing the windows for another moment. He stared beyond the parking lot to the bay on the far side of the highway. The wind was brutal today, stirring the surface of the water choppy and rough. The view was shades of gray between the clouds and water. In a flash, he sensed Janie's presence. His body was that attuned to her. He turned to find her walking in his direction. When she reached him, her eyes looked uncertain.

Before she had a chance to speak, he did, barreling through the muddle inside. "Let's grab some dinner tonight," he blurted out.

Her gorgeous hazel eyes widened before she nodded. "I was just about to ask if you got my text." At his nod, she continued. "My mom took Stella and Pansy to Anchorage for the night."

"Well, why don't we grab dinner at the Boathouse?" he asked, latching onto the first restaurant that came to mind.

"Perfect. Should I meet…?"

"I'll pick you up," he said firmly.

They stood there for another few beats. Hot lust jolted through him just to have her near. It wasn't even noon yet, and he had hours to go before he could have her to himself. It was so bad, he was mentally considering the idea of yanking her down one of the aisles just to snatch a chance to feel her lips under his again. With a mental shake, he grabbed his stack of mail. "Six o'clock sound good?" he asked abruptly.

At her nod, he spun away and nearly stalked out of the post office. He was far from upset, but he was rattled by how strongly she affected him.

* * *

Janie stood in the bathroom, her reflection staring back at her in the mirror. Born and raised in Alaska, she was a relentlessly practical woman and dressed mostly with the weather in mind, not her appearance. Given her strong inclination to avoid men at all costs ever since watching what Randy did to her mother, she'd skipped over the common adolescent anxieties about how she looked. She grabbed the hairbrush again and whipped it through her hair. Her hair was, well, it was brown. At the moment, it was also quite shiny because she'd brushed it enough it practically glowed. She kept it just past her shoulders in a layered cut. It tended to wave slightly, and she was annoyed with a particular wave that kept curling out no matter what she did. *You're being ridiculous. Travis will be here any minute and you've spent forever on your hair.*

With an abrupt sigh, she slammed the hairbrush on the counter. She quickly swiped lip-gloss on and stomped out of the bathroom. She'd already wasted plenty of time obsessing over what to wear, only to settle on a pair of jeans and a soft green scoop neck shirt. When she couldn't decide what to wear, she'd figured it made the most sense to go with something comfortable. There was also the problem of having few clothes that were anything other than practical.

There was a knock on the kitchen door as she stepped off the stairs. She hurried to the door and swung it open. "Hey! Just let me grab my coat." She was talking rapidly, her anxiety ramping her up inside. She'd come to the crazy conclusion she was going to get Travis out of her system for once and for all tonight. Translation: she planned to screw his brains out before she lost her mind. A few awkward dates and sexual experiences and hardly any in recent memory left her stirred up and tossed wildly in the storm of the desire. Travis's presence didn't do much to settle her nerves, in fact it sent every nerve scrambling.

She grabbed her lightweight down jacket and tugged it on, stuffing her feet into a pair of lined leather boots at the same time. When she glanced up, Travis's blue eyes were on her. In a flash, heat raced through her. His eyes were like the ocean, changing shades of blue that mesmerized her. "Okay, ready!" she said brightly.

One corner of his mouth curled up in a half grin. "Okay then. Let's go."

She followed him out into the night. The sky was clear, the air sharp and crisp. The chill outside eased the heat swirling inside of her. In short order, they were standing inside the crowded waiting area of The Boathouse Café. The pace was slower in the winter, but it was still busy. Janie glanced around and saw many unfamiliar faces mixed in with locals. The Boathouse was a local and tourist favorite. Ever since Last Frontier Lodge, a local ski resort, had reopened, the tourists were in Diamond Creek year-round. Travis had thought ahead and made a reservation, so they were seated within minutes of their arrival.

Dinner passed in a strange blur for her. In some ways, it was quite normal. She managed to eat and carry on a casual conversation. She even managed to greet a few friends who stopped by their table to say hello. Travis bantered with Luke Winters when he stopped by their table with his wife Hannah, an old friend of Janie's. Janie glanced up at Hannah, tall and willowy with sky blue eyes and a warm smile. "How's it going?" Janie asked.

Hannah smiled, her eyes flicking from Janie to Travis and back again, mild curiosity in her gaze. "Busy, but good. How about you?"

Janie shrugged. "About the same. Not sure if you heard, but Stella broke her ankle in a sledding accident, so we've been dealing with that. Otherwise, John's doing great in class. He's full of energy and he loves to ask questions," she said, referring to Hannah and Luke's son who had started in her first grade class this year.

Hannah laughed softly. "You really do know how to spin the positive. He is so full of energy, he wears me out, and he never stops asking questions. I can't tell you how glad I am that you're his teacher."

Janie laughed. Given that she felt muddled and like she was walking blind through whatever this was with Travis, a few moments of talking about teaching settled her. Having grown up with Hannah, she knew her well enough to know Hannah was probably wondering about her and Travis. Janie didn't think much about the fact she rarely dated, but it felt like a glaring detail right now. Travis was laughing along with something Luke said. Hannah's eyes flicked between them again. She curled her hand over the edge of Janie's chair and leaned down.

"He's good for you," Hannah said, her voice low and barely audible over the murmur of conversation around them.

Janie glanced up, suddenly vulnerable and off-kilter again. Hannah's warm blue eyes met hers, and she gave Janie's shoulder a quick squeeze before straightening up when Luke curled his arm across her shoulders. They said their goodbyes and strolled away. Hannah slipped her hand in the rear pocket of Luke's jeans, while he idly sifted his hand through her dark hair. Their casual intimacy struck Janie, sending a flash of longing through her. She'd watched many friends find love, yet she'd never questioned her commitment to staying single. Until Travis. She glanced over at him. He turned as their waiter approached. The lines of his profile were clean and strong. Her breath caught and her heart gave a hard thump before her pulse took off at a gallop.

*T*ravis adjusted an armful of firewood as he climbed the steps to the porch. While they'd been at dinner, the temperature had dropped dramatically. It was already cold, yet it had dipped lower into the teeth-chattering range. He nudged the kitchen door with his knee and stepped inside, toeing his boots off by the door, as they were damp from the crunchy snow in Janie's yard.

"Here we go," he said as he approached the fireplace in her living room.

Janie reached over and quickly took half of what he carried, turning to lay the logs in the fireplace. He set the remainder in the wrought-iron rack beside the fireplace and stepped back while she strategically placed a few pieces of tinder under the logs and lit a piece of paper, which she slipped in between the tinder and logs as soon as it caught fire.

There was a soft hissing sound and then the tinder lit up, flames rippling through the logs. Janie was leaning over, her gaze on the fire. Travis could hardly keep his eyes off the lush curves of her hips. He'd managed to get through dinner without completely losing control of himself, but he was about at the end of his tether, his restraint hanging on by a thin thread and sheer will.

She stood and turned to face him. Her dark hair fell in loose waves around her shoulders. Her porcelain skin was flushed slightly and her eyes bright. He couldn't say he'd thought much about what to do next. He recalled Nathan's comment that he should do something about Janie. So, he'd asked her to dinner, only to learn dinner with Janie teased him to near madness. Here with her now, lust rolled through him in a flash. He gave up thinking and closed the distance between them in one long stride. Her head angled up to him when he reached her. He forced himself to hold still, barely able to hear over the fast pounding of his heart. Even if his control was almost lost, he wanted to give her a chance to back away. She didn't take it. She simply watched him, her layered hazel eyes dark with desire. Her pulse fluttered in her neck. The sound of her breathing, shallow and soft, sent him over the edge. He threaded a hand in her hair and dipped his head forward to fit his mouth over hers.

She was still for a beat and then sighed against his lips. That was it. He was lost. He swept his tongue into her mouth, reveling at her response. Their kiss went from hot to searing in seconds—a tangle of lips and tongue. She met him stroke for stroke. The fire beside them snapped and crackled, heat starting to emanate nearby, while the fire between them was nearly all consuming. He sifted his hand through her hair and down her spine, tracing the dip of her waist and the generous curve of her bottom. He couldn't resist pulling her against him, groaning into her mouth at the feel of her softness against his hardness. He needed more and he needed it now. He tore his lips free and gulped in air before blazing a wet trail of kisses along the column of her throat and her collarbone.

While he was busy exploring the sweet taste of her skin, she was busy with her own exploration. One hand stroked up his chest and down his back, while the other reached between them to curl over his cock —rock hard and throbbing. He growled against her skin and lifted his head. He met her eyes in the flickering firelight. He grabbed onto what little control he had left and forced himself to breathe. "Janie," he said roughly.

Her eyes were dark and she gave a small nod.

"If you want us to stop, we need to stop now." He bit the words out, forcing himself to hold on. He didn't want to push her further than she wanted to go, but he seriously didn't know how much he could take before he lost what little control he had.

She gave a tiny shake of her head. Uncertain what that meant, he held her eyes. "What do you mean?"

She licked her lips. *Holy hell.* If she meant for him to keep some semblance of control, she needed not to do things like that. "I don't want to stop," she replied, her voice husky.

That was all he needed. He stroked his palms down her sides and curled his hands around her hips, lifting her against him. In a few strides, he was by the couch and sat down with her in his arms. She was a bundle of softness and curves. Her eyes slammed into his and she shifted to straddle him. "This," she said, the roughness in her voice sending a hot jolt through him as she brought her mouth to his again.

* * *

JANIE FOUND herself sitting astride Travis, the feel of his hot length grazing against her with every subtle shift of her hips. She was teetering on the edge of pure madness. She'd decided she would let herself have this, yet *this* with Travis went beyond anything she could have anticipated. The wild pounding beat of desire between them had ratcheted up to a burning conflagration. Sometime in the last few minutes, he'd made quick work of her shirt and bra, while she'd shoved his shirt off. Amidst kisses and a tangled scramble, he'd tugged her jeans down where they dangled from an ankle. She gave a kick to free them and settled against him, a moan escaping at the feel of his hard cock through the damp silk of her panties. The denim was rough against the silk and she savored the friction.

A luscious shiver raced through her when he dipped his head and swirled his tongue around a nipple taut with need. She gasped with relief at the feel of his mouth on her bare skin. A subtle suction before he pulled away elicited a sharp cry. She gripped his hair when he shifted his attention to the other nipple, tracing wet circles with his fingers when he lifted his head. He held her gaze as he reached down and dragged his fingers along her low belly before hooking over the edge of her panties and delving down.

Barely able to breathe, her eyes fell closed as he stroked into her folds. She was drenched with need, her channel throbbing and slick. Her breath came in soft gasps, and she teetered on a delicious edge. Spun tight inside, his slow strokes into her channel only served to tighten the coil. He said her name, his voice low and gruff. She managed to drag her eyes open to find his waiting. Another finger joined the first, stretching her and sending hot streaks of pleasure through her. She was caught in his dark blue gaze and couldn't look away as he began to rhythmically stroke into her. Her hips rolled into his touch as the pressure gathered within. In a flash, the sensation built to a crescendo. She distantly heard herself cry out sharply when his thumb circled over her clit, and then the pressure let loose, crashing over her in waves of intense pleasure.

He stilled his fingers and slowly dragged them out. Even though she was nearly boneless, she knew she wanted more. She shifted her hips back and tore at his jeans, tugging them down around his hips swiftly and sighing when his cock sprung free. Curling her hand around his length, she closed her eyes at the feel of his hot, velvety skin. She felt him shift and glanced up to see him fumbling in his pocket. He swore softly and tossed his wallet aside once he yanked a condom out. She grabbed it from him and tore the packet open. In seconds, she'd rolled it on and rose up.

"Janie."

Her eyes collided with his just as he curled a hand around her hip and held her still. Restless, she shifted her hips, but he held firm. He positioned his cock at her entrance, her channel clenching with need at the subtle pressure. In slow motion, he eased her down, his cock filling and stretching her slowly. As she sank onto him, she bucked against his grip at the last moment, sinking deeply against him. The sensation of him inside of her felt so damn good, she lost her breath.

They were still together for a long moment, yet inside she was spiraling with need. The echoes of her climax rustled within, pleasure rising in small bursts as she settled against him—the hard, hot length of him pulsing subtly. She gathered herself and rose up, almost crying out at the slow slide of him within. They rocked together, slow at first and gradually picking up the pace until she felt as if she was hurtling into madness again. He tangled a hand in her hair and pulled her close, claiming her mouth in a fierce kiss. The charge humming through her became hotter and hotter as she chased another sweet release.

With every stroke of him inside, the wildness built until he gripped her hips and brought her down hard against him as he surged to meet her. Another surge and the pleasure broke loose again, streaking through her in waves as her channel convulsed around him. He caught her cry in their kiss, tearing his lips free as he threw his head back against the couch, his body going taut against hers. He slowly relaxed, his hands loosening on her hips. All she wanted was to stay right there, so she let her head fall forward into the dip of his shoulder and caught her breath. She idly traced the hard muscled planes of his chest, marveling at how good it felt to be this close to him. His body was a work of art, but it wasn't just that. It was the shimmering incandescent feeling between them. After several long moments, she lifted her head. He rolled his head to the side where it had fallen back on the couch.

"You're getting cold," he said softly, running a hand

up her back, his touch alerting her to the goose bumps on her skin.

* * *

TRAVIS CAME AWAKE SLOWLY. For a second, he was confused when he felt soft curves against him. Then, he remembered where he was—in Janie's bed. He opened his eyes to find Janie sound asleep beside him. Her dark hair was tangled on the pillow. The winter dawn was just breaking, wispy light filtering through the curtains in her bedroom. Without moving, he slowly scanned the room, which he'd stumbled into in the dark late last night. There was a dormer window on one side and a picture window offering a view of the bay on the other side. The curtains hung open in the center, revealing the snow falling softly outside. Janie's bed was a queen-size four-poster bed of dark mahogany. Ample pillows and a fluffy down quilt made for an incredibly comfortable night's sleep. There was that and the most incredible sex he'd ever had last night—two factors contributing to him feeling very well rested this morning. Well, and Janie's lush curves and silky skin against him. She was curled beside him with one of her legs tangled in his. She shifted just the slightest bit, and his cock responded.

He almost laughed. He didn't want her to think all he wanted was sex, but it was hard not to think about that almost all the time with her. His body was like a tuning fork with her, attuned to everything about her. He forced himself to take a deep breath, trying to wrestle control of his body. Her leg slid against his again, sending another hot jolt of lust through him. Damn. He was in deep.

CHAPTER 13

"*D*anny! Back in your seat," Janie called out. She watched as Danny literally bounced back into his seat from several desks over. She had to bite back a laugh. Danny was a little bundle of energy, but his good-natured attitude saved him from being an annoyance. She scanned the class, checking to make sure she had some semblance of attention from most of the students. "Okay, let's vote on the marker color for the afternoon! Danny, you're in charge of counting hands," she said with a quick nod in his direction. Danny immediately wiggled his bottom in his seat and grabbed the small erase board and marker on his desk. "Hands up for red," she announced. She quickly ran through the options for green, blue and yellow and then looked to Danny. "Okay, what'll it be this afternoon?"

Danny, his brown eyes alert, looked up. "Yellow and blue are tied."

"Okay, tie-breaker vote. Yellow?" she asked the room at large. Hands shot up. She gave Danny enough time to count and record the answer before moving on. "Blue?" Once Danny looked up, she arched a brow.

"Blue! That's my favorite!" Danny announced with a wiggle and a grin.

One of her small tricks to keep kids engaged in class was her twice-daily vote on which color marker she used on the board. It was a tiny thing, but many tiny things like that helped her students feel included. She picked up her blue marker and moved onto the afternoon lessons for math and language arts. After the last bell rang and her students gathered their backpacks and scrambled out of her classroom, she sank down at her desk.

One thing she loved about teaching was it kept her mind engaged, although today had been a day of almost constant distraction. She'd managed, but just barely, to pay attention. All day long, thoughts of Travis had feathered along the edges of her mind. The other night had almost consumed her, in more ways than one. There was the simple truth that she'd never lost herself with anyone the way she lost herself with him. It had been nothing but a blur of pure sensation and connection. Waking up beside him had been a slice of heaven she'd never imagined. She'd offered to make omelets for breakfast, and he'd surprised her by jumping in to help and demonstrating he was a more than adequate cook. He'd had to leave after an emergency call to a moose collision on the highway. She'd had her annoyances with moose over the years, but it was a first to be annoyed because they interrupted her morning with a man. Stella arrived home with Pansy in a bustle of excitement about her mini-shopping trip with her grandmother. Janie had somehow managed to collect herself and behave normally, all the while her body was still reverberating from the night with Travis.

It was Monday now, and Travis had called twice and texted several times. He clearly seemed to get, without stating it explicitly, that ensconcing himself in her life with Stella wasn't the simplest thing to do. Yet, he made it clear he wanted to see her. Soon. Often. She flushed straight through just thinking about the feel of him inside of her. She gave her head a quick shake and gathered the loose papers on her desk together.

"Hey there, thought I'd find you here."

Janie glanced up to find Tess Winters at the doorway. "Hey Tess! What brings you here?"

Tess was a newer friend since she'd only moved to Diamond Creek a few years ago, but they'd gotten close. She'd helped Janie organize a school fundraiser the first month she officially moved to Diamond Creek after falling head over heels in love with Nathan Winters. They'd become fast friends then. Janie appreciated Tess's no-nonsense, practical approach to life and work, and her sly sense of humor. Tess stepped into the classroom, swinging her purse from her hand. "Oh, I had a meeting with Nancy about organizing the annual fundraiser for the music program. Seeing as the bell just rang, I figured you'd still be around."

Tess plunked down in a desk across from Janie's, her petite frame looking large in the small child-size desk. She brushed a honey-brown curl out of her eyes and met Janie's gaze. "What's up with you? We need to get together for dinner soon."

"How about tonight?" Janie asked, startling herself.

Her question wasn't unusual, but she was taken aback by the urgency she felt inside. She was desperate for some feedback on the doubts rampaging through her about Travis.

Tess pulled her phone out and quickly texted someone. She set it down on the desk with a smile. "Just texted Nathan to tell him he's on his own for dinner. How much you wanna bet he goes over to one of his brother's for dinner now?"

Janie chuckled. "Not worth the bet because that's almost a guarantee, right?"

Tess threw her head back with a laugh. "Yup. He's actually pretty decent around the kitchen, but he's got two sisters-in-law who are phenomenal cooks, so it's a win if he stops by for dinner. Anyway, let's do an early happy hour. I'm not up for anything late because it's too damn cold out."

"Me neither. Sally's?" Janie asked, referring to a local favorite restaurant and bar.

"Perfect. You ready or do you need a few minutes?"

Janie slid the papers into a file folder and put them away in her desk drawer. "Ready," she said as she stood and pulled her coat off the back of her chair.

Tess followed her over to Sally's, a short drive from the elementary school. With a chilly wind gusting across the parking lot, they jogged inside together, a swirl of air following them through the door. Sally's was in an old renovated barn. The kitchen was in the center of the space with the bar and an area for live music on one side and the restaurant on the other. Janie and Tess snagged the last booth available.

Once they were seated and had ordered drinks,

Tess looked over at Janie. "What's up? You seem, I don't know, worried about something."

Janie leaned back with a sigh. "Can't we start with some small talk?"

Tess's ginger eyes crinkled at the corners with her laugh. "Nope. I know you too well."

"Okay, fine. I've been seeing Travis Wilkes and I don't know what the hell to do about it."

A slow smile spread across Tess's face. "I heard you went to dinner with him, so I was wondering what was up with that. Travis is a good guy, and he's pretty easy on the eyes. Maybe you should just relax and see what happens."

Janie rolled her eyes and started to reply when their waitress arrived with their drinks. After she served them and took their dinner order, Janie took a sip of her wine and glanced over at Tess again. "You know I don't really date, so it's kind of a thing that I'm seeing anyone. At all."

Tess nodded. "Right. I know you haven't dated anyone the whole time I've lived here. I kept meaning to ask why, but you seemed so okay with it all that I never got around to it. Don't suppose you could clue me in on why?"

Janie realized that even though she and Tess were close, Tess didn't know about her mother's history and Janie's painful brush with Randy's fist. Come to think of it, she'd never really spelled out to anyone why she avoided relationships. It had been an unconscious choice at first and then after a few attempts at dating, she'd realized she didn't think it was worth the worry and bother. Sex hadn't been unpleasant, but it hadn't blown her away either. Except for the other night with Travis—she was still reeling from that, little shocks rippling through her body whenever she thought about it. She looked over at Tess and gathered her thoughts.

"It's an old story, which is probably why you haven't heard it, but my mom's boyfriend after my dad died turned out to be an abusive jerk. She didn't manage to get away from him until he broke my jaw." When Tess's eyes widened, Janie gave a shrug. "It was awful, but I'm fine and he's long gone. But I guess it made me think relationships weren't worth it. I mean, how do you know who's worth trusting? When my mom started dating Randy, he seemed like a decent guy. By the end of it all, she barely left the house, and he hauled off and punched me for talking back. I prefer being independent to worrying about relationships."

Tess's eyes were bright, but steely. "Look, nobody should have to go through that." She paused as if considering her words. "I get it. I totally get why you might think it's the smart choice to avoid relationships. I'm not one of those people who thinks everyone needs to pair up, but if your choice to be alone is to avoid something, then it's not really a choice. There are no guarantees. Ever. But I can tell you Travis isn't that guy. He's been friends with Nathan for years. There's all kinds of things I don't know about him, but I'm damn sure he's not an abusive jerk."

Janie stared over at Tess and absorbed her words. Intellectually, she knew Tess made sense and it was what she'd tell a friend if the situation were reversed. She took a deep breath and let it out slowly, idly spinning her wineglass in her hand. "I get it and just the fact I went to dinner with Travis more than once should tell you I'm trying not to let that weird logic get in the way. I guess I just don't know what the hell to do. All this time I was okay alone because no one ever came along and made me want more."

Tess arched a brow. "Aha. So that's it. Well, I can't talk reason to you on that," she offered with a soft laugh. "I was half-crazy when I met Nathan. You didn't meet me until after I got over being ridiculous over him. All I can say is hang in there. Maybe it helps if I mention I think Travis is about as worked up as you."

"He is?" Her heart gave a swift kick.

At Janie's question, Tess burst out laughing. "Oh, you have it bad!"

Their waitress arrived, quickly served their burgers, topped off their drinks and spun away. Janie was relieved to have a moment to get her blush under control. After she had a bite of her salmon burger, she looked across the table at Tess. "So what do you mean by that?"

Tess finished chewing and took a sip of water. "He was over at our place the other week and when I guessed you were the woman he had dinner with, he got all flustered. Nathan mentioned last week that he thought Travis was serious about you and had no idea what to do. They're pretty tight, and you know Nathan, he's always teasing. I'm sure he gave Travis some grief about you, and Travis must've gotten worked up over it."

Janie's heart gave a little spin to think Travis might be as rattled as she was. She took another bite of her burger. Tess nibbled on a sweet potato fry and looked over at her, a gleam in her eyes. "So you like him. A lot," she said flatly.

Janie's cheeks heated—again—before a giggle escaped. "Obviously I do. I didn't manage to avoid dating for years without finally giving into someone I don't like. That's the whole problem. I like him. A lot." Her words startled her. They were quite true—that itself was shocking for her. She'd come to value her independence and hadn't ever considered it a form of avoidance. Maybe it wasn't. It was just that she wasn't used to being this drawn to a man and feeling so vulnerable inside.

Tess finished off her burger and took a sip of water, followed by wine. "Honestly, I hadn't thought about the two of you together, but now that I have, I'm glad to see you're not chasing him off. Travis is one of the good guys. I don't spend much time thinking about Nathan's friends, but Travis is the kind of man worth waiting for. He's nice, he's smart, he's a good friend, and even if he's not my cup of tea, he's damn sexy." A sly smile followed her last comment.

Janie burst out laughing before sobering. "Well, I guess I'm glad you can vouch for him."

Tess leaned forward. "Seriously. Maybe he hasn't had any serious relationship I know about, but as far as the kind of friend he is, he's rock solid. Aside from his brothers, Travis is probably the only guy I know who Nathan would call in the middle of the night if he needed something. No doubt in my mind, Travis would be there for what he needed. Plus, seeing as he's an emergency responder, he's super helpful in dicey situations."

"I know. He fished me out of the bay. That's how this whole thing started."

Tess grinned. "Oh right. Forgot all about that."

Their waitress arrived to check on them after which the conversation moved onto less emotionally fraught territory for Janie. Later that evening, Stella sprawled on the couch with Pansy curled up beside her, and Janie fed another log into the fireplace. She stood and looked over at Stella, her heart squeezing a little. Her small family felt like a hard won battle. Stella had been so prickly and guarded at first. Yet now, several years past her adoption, it felt as if she'd always been Janie's daughter. While Janie adored her own family, the short years with Randy in her mother's life had made her yearn for nothing more than peace in her home. She believed Travis was trustworthy, yet she still wasn't so sure what it might mean to let him into her life.

"Hey Trav!" Ben called.

Travis glanced up from where he was waiting in the cherry picker, the bucket mounted to the lift on the fire truck. The crew had been called to a fire at a residence on the far side of town. They'd arrived to find all of the residents safe, but the daughter had been crying and nearly inconsolable over her dogs trapped upstairs. He and Ben had volunteered to try to save them. The fire had started in the woodstove, which happened to be beside the stairs. As such, the only way to get upstairs to rescue the dogs was with the handy cherry picker. Travis had already crawled in and pulled one dog out. The dog in question sat panting by his feet in the cherry picker, while Ben was now returning with the other dog.

Travis adjusted the controls on the cherry picker and eased as close as he could to the other window. Once he was within reach, he leaned over and carefully lifted the dog from Ben's arms. As soon as he had the dog in the bucket, Ben crawled through the window and joined them. Travis silently thanked the stars for the two dogs being calm enough to make the rescue manageable. After they were lowered down, he climbed out to have Ben pass the dogs over. One by one, the dogs were set on the ground and ran straight to the little girl, two wiggling black bundles of joy. The fire had largely been put out by this point, so Travis helped the crew finish up.

When he turned to head to the fire truck again, he stopped when he felt a small tug on his leg. He looked down to find the little girl looking up at him with wide brown eyes. Her eyes were still puffy from crying, but nothing other than joy shone in them now. "Wiggly and Squiggly say thank you," she said solemnly.

Travis knelt beside her and reached out to stroke his hands over the dogs, both of whom were glued to the little girl's side. "No problem. We knew we could get them out safe, and here they are. How are you doing?" he asked, his eyes coasting over her. She was practically swallowed up in an adult's jacket, likely borrowed from someone once the family got out safely.

"I'm good! Daddy says we have lots of work to do before we can move back in, but no one got hurt and that's all that matters."

"You're absolutely right about that. Let's go find your parents," he said as he stood and held a hand out.

A while later, he stepped into the shower at the fire station and sighed as the steaming water ran over him. He was on duty for another few hours, but he needed to wash off the grit and grime from the last fire. Janie had been dancing through his thoughts for days and sashayed into his mind just now. The other night with her had taken him places he'd never been, nor considered possible. He forced his thoughts off of her. The last thing he needed was to start fantasizing about her while he was showering at work. Moments later after he'd barely finished getting dressed and was lacing up his boots, his radio buzzed. The police were calling for the ambulance to respond to a domestic dispute. He snatched his gear and raced downstairs, climbing into the ambulance beside Ben at the last second.

"Thought you might miss this call," Ben commented as he turned on the siren and sped down the highway.

"Almost did, but I'm here," Travis replied. "Know anything about the domestic dispute?"

At that moment, their radios sounded in unison, first repeating the address. What came next sent a flash of anger through Travis, so raw his fists clenched unconsciously. "Police are apprehending a Randy Price. Sixty-year old Caucasian male with known history of violence and criminal record. Most recently arrested for a domestic assault in Fairbanks. Reportedly fled the area. Call came in an hour ago from his girlfriend who reports he assaulted her and locked her in the shed. Police responded and Mr. Price had an altercation with one of the officers. Both sustained injuries."

Travis's chest tightened and his anger ran from cold to hot in a flash. "Let's get there," he said, his voice low.

Ben glanced sideways. "On the way, pushing seventy right now, so hold tight," he said as he rounded a curve in the highway and turned onto a winding road leading up a hillside.

Within minutes, they pulled into the driveway of the residence with another cop car spinning into the drive in front of them. It was all Travis could do to hold back, but they weren't to enter the scene without clearance from the police. He saw Darren lift a hand in a wave, gesturing toward an area where there were two trucks. The home was in ramshackle condition with no siding on it, torn weather sheathing flapping in the wind, and tarps tied onto the roof, likely to prevent leaking. There were several small outbuildings in the same condition. Travis saw a woman being led out of a shed. She was shivering so badly, he could see her shake from a distance. He pulled his radio off his shoulder. "Sylvia, we need another ambulance up here. Aside from the two injuries reported, there's a woman who looks to be hypothermic, depending on how long she's been outside."

Sylvia's reply was swift. "Already sent the next one right behind you guys."

He heard the siren approaching as she spoke. Ben caught his eye. "Let's get to the injuries first."

In seconds, they reached the trucks where the officers on scene were gathered. The injured officer was sitting on the ground and leaning against one of the truck tires. The man Travis guessed to be Randy Price lay several feet away on his side with cuffs holding his hands together behind his back. Travis hadn't said a word to Ben about Randy Price, but Ben seemed to know it might not be the best plan for Travis to handle him. "I've got Randy. You help him," Ben said firmly.

Travis stopped in his tracks. "No, I..."

Ben shook his head sharply. "I know exactly who

Randy is and so do you. I might think he's an asshole, but it's not personal."

Travis took a sharp breath and nodded, his anger easing slightly. "Fine." He spun away and strode to the officer. Travis realized it was Charlie Brooks, the police chief's main partner and a long-time officer on the force. Charlie's expression was a mix of annoyance and pain. His blue eyes were resigned when Travis knelt at his side. "Hey man, how's it going?" Charlie asked, his tone strained.

"Better than you probably," Travis replied. "What's up with your shoulder?" he asked, nodding toward the shoulder Charlie held with one hand.

Charlie blew a puff of air out, blowing his brown hair out of his eyes. "Dislocated it. Hurts like hell. At least Randy's in cuffs."

"Mind letting me take a look?" he asked.

Charlie let his hand fall away. Travis quickly felt over the shoulder, which was definitely dislocated. A minor injury, but rather painful. He caught Charlie's eyes. "It's dislocated alright. What happened?"

Charlie breathed in sharply when Travis carefully rolled Charlie's shoulder between his palms, but he responded without missing a beat. "I'm sure you heard his girlfriend called to report he'd punched her and locked her in the shed. He's not the brightest bulb, so he didn't think to take her phone away. She called from the shed, but not before she'd been out for enough time that she was damn near freezing when we got here. It was quiet when we arrived. So quiet, we weren't sure he was still here. Next thing we knew, Randy comes flying around the corner there..." He paused and angled his head toward the corner of the house. "...and his fists were flying. Not sure exactly how I messed my shoulder up, but it happened when he tripped and took me to the ground with him. Bummer for him, he landed on his knee on a rusty old trap. Tore his knee up good." Charlie shook his head. "Am I right that it's gonna hurt worse for you to put my shoulder back in place than it did when it popped out?'

Travis nodded and glanced up when another team reached them with a stretcher for Charlie. Charlie looked from Travis to the stretcher. "Seriously guys, I can walk. It's just my shoulder."

Travis eyed him and shrugged. "Don't know if that's true, or if it's more that you know what's coming." Charlie was distracted when someone called out to Darren. When he looked away, Travis made sure he had the right hold on Charlie's shoulder and moved swiftly, realigning the shoulder ball into the socket.

Charlie whipped his head back, his breath hissing through his teeth. He tensed and then relaxed. "Okay, not so bad. I'm guessing it's gonna be sore as hell for a bit."

Travis nodded. "Oh yeah. We'll get a sling on it for now. We should still get you to the hospital for a quick check. I wanted to try to get it in place now before it swelled up. The doctor can do a more thorough check and maybe give you a specialized splint if you need it. Think you can stand?"

Charlie rolled his eyes. "Of course I can stand." Belying his dismissive comment, he took Travis's hand when offered and came to his feet with a grunt.

Travis walked him to the ambulance and fit a sling on Charlie's arm, leaving him to wait with one of the other officers for a moment. He looked over to where

Ben and two other emergency responders were tending to Randy. He itched to go over there. Just as he started to move in their direction, a hand curled around his arm. He glanced back to see Darren. He started to shake his arm free, but Darren held firm. "I'm sure you've got some thoughts about Randy, but now is definitely not the time."

Travis shook his arm free, swearing under his breath. "What is it with everyone keeping me away from him?"

Darren held his gaze for a moment and shook his head incrementally. "Maybe you're stupid, but I'm not. Randy's got years of bad history with Janie's mom and it ended with his fist in Janie's face. The last thing we need right now is you pissed off at him in the middle of a call that has nothing to do with Janie."

Travis knew Darren was right, but he didn't like it one bit. He shifted his shoulders and busied himself by tidying his supplies and putting them away. He glanced back to Darren. "Seeing as I've barely talked about Janie, how come you and Ben are worrying about how I might respond to Randy?"

Darren rolled his eyes. "Dude, this town's small and word travels." With another shake of his head, he strode away toward where Ben and the other team were wheeling the stretcher to the second ambulance.

Later that afternoon, Travis climbed into his truck. He'd had enough sense to start it a few minutes ago, so it was getting warm inside. He drove away, his mind spinning over thoughts of Janie. He'd had to fight the urge to come up with a reason to stop by the hospital. The only reason he wanted to stop by was to track Randy down. He knew it didn't make a lick of sense to find the guy for the sole reason of knocking his lights out, but that's what Travis wanted to do. He hated knowing that any man was violent towards the women in their life, but knowing what Randy did to Janie made it far more personal.

Her warmth, her steely strength, her unconscious sexiness and just about everything about her tugged at his heart, so hard he didn't know how to handle his feelings. He abruptly turned into the post office parking lot and jogged inside to grab his mail. Snow was starting to fall again, coming in fits and starts, but slowly picking up its pace. He brushed the snow out of his hair when he stepped into the post office and glanced around. As usual, there was a line to the counter. He strode quickly down the aisle to his post office box and was walking back, sifting mail in his hands, when he heard his name.

Before he looked up, he knew it was Janie. The sound of her voice was seared into his brain now. She stood a few feet away, her hand held on the key to what must be her post office box. Her hand fell away, and she turned to face him. Her hair was damp from the snow, her cheeks flushed and her eyes bright.

They stood still, simply staring at each other for a few beats, before Janie finally spoke. "Hey."

It felt as if the air around them was charged, humming with desire. He tried to speak, but nothing came out. He cleared his throat. "Hey there. I'd ask what you're up to, but I'm guessing you're getting the mail."

Her lips curled in a smile. "Yup. Getting the mail. 'Spose that's what you're doing too."

He nodded, trying to wrangle the lust coursing through him under control. He wasn't accustomed to this wild pounding need Janie elicited in him. She lifted a hand and brushed a loose lock of hair out of her eyes. The small, unconscious motion sent another jolt of need through him. Without thinking, he stepped closer and caught her hand in his as she lowered it. It was cool, and he curled his palm around it. Her breath hitched. His eyes landed on the rapid flutter of her pulse in her neck before traveling up to her mouth—lush and pink from the chill outside. Before he could form a thought, he dipped his head and fit his mouth over hers.

Another step and she was flush against him. He tangled a hand in her hair and stroked down her back to cup her bottom. He lost all sense of where they were, solely focused on her. Her tongue stroked against his, and she flexed in his embrace. Desperate for more, he trailed kisses along her jaw and her neck, the skin soft with a hint of sweet. She was like a drug —the feel of her lush curves against him, the taste of her skin, the soft pants escaping from her. He was nearly out of his mind when a loud thump broke through the haze of passion fogging his mind. He lifted his head and glanced around, suddenly aware of where they were. No one happened to be in the aisle. He figured someone must've dropped something the next aisle over.

He looked down to find Janie's eyes on him. Clouded with passion, her gaze locked onto his. He was rock-hard and wished he could take her right here. Unbidden, his eyes dropped lower, as if magnet-ically drawn. Her breasts rose and fell with her rapid breathing. She wore another one of those scoop-neck shirts where the collar dipped to reveal the tops of her breasts. He hadn't realized he was cupping one of her breasts in his palm, his thumb tracing back and forth over her taut nipple. The sound of footsteps coming their way nudged a little more sense into his brain. He had to force his hand to still and slowly let it slide down.

She took a small step back, creating a tiny bit of space between them. When he met her eyes again, he was relieved to see she looked as dazed as he felt.

* * *

JANIE STARED AT TRAVIS, almost losing herself again in the blur of his blue gaze. Her heart was pounding, her belly was swirling with need, and she was drenched. To make matters even more confounding, they were standing in the post office with privacy nowhere in sight and all she wanted was to be skin to skin with him. She gave herself a mental shake, a feeble effort to gain control of her body. The murmur of voices from the counter area several aisles away filtered through finally. Footsteps echoed on the tiled floor in the aisle adjacent to them.

She forced herself to take a slow breath and took another step back, almost physically pained when his hand loosened in her hair and his other hand slid away. More footsteps sounded and then turned down the aisle where they stood. Still struggling to catch her breath, she looked over at Travis. "Do you want to come over for dinner tomorrow?"

She asked the question without thinking about it. All she knew was she wanted to see him. Now. Unfortunately, now meant rushing back to the house to pick up Stella and take her to recital practice. With the holidays in full swing, Stella had several performances coming up, so practices were scheduled nightly and tended to run late.

"Don't suppose I could invite myself over tonight?" he countered with a grin.

A wash of heat rolled through her, and she grinned. She felt almost giddy with delight that he didn't want to wait. She shook her head with a little laugh. "Stella has recital, so I'll be in the auditorium for hours grading papers."

He held her eyes for a long moment, sending another wash of heat through her, before nodding firmly. "Got it. Tomorrow it is. Should I bring anything?"

"You brought pizza last time. I'll cook. Any preferences?"

"I'll eat anything."

Someone called Travis's name and he looked beyond her. "Hey Ben," he commented.

Janie turned to see the firefighter who'd been with Travis dealing with the errant moose on the playground. She knew Ben in passing, but that was all. He reached them, twirling his keys on his index finger as he spoke. "Hey there. Feels like I've been with you all day," he said by way of greeting.

Travis rolled his eyes. "You pretty much have."

Ben glanced to Janie. "How's it going Janie?"

Though her body was still suffused with heat from her searing kiss with Travis and his mere presence, she managed to smile politely. "Oh fine. Just getting my mail."

She spun to finish the task she'd started before she saw Travis. Opening her mailbox, she pulled out the small handful of envelopes and closed the box. Ben was saying something to Travis in a low voice, and her ears perked up.

"…in surgery now. Darren already filed charges, so no worries, he won't be going anywhere once he's out of the hospital."

She couldn't say why, but her gut coiled. Clutching her mail tightly in her hand, she turned to face them. "What happened?"

Travis's eyes slammed into hers, worry in their depths. Ben glanced from her to Travis and back. They were both silent for long enough, she became annoyed. "Guys, really? I know you deal with emergencies all the time. Who's in surgery and why?"

Travis watched her for another moment and ran a hand through his hair. "Randy Price is back in town. The police got a call about a domestic incident. Long story short, he got into an altercation with Charlie Brooks. Randy fell on a rusty trap and tore his knee up."

His explanation was simple and concise. Janie had never spoken to Travis about Randy, but she knew by the expression on his face that he knew who he was to her. Ben had been around during those years, so she knew without a doubt he knew the entire sordid tale. She felt like she'd been punched in the gut. Randy had been away from Diamond Creek for years, but she'd never managed to completely erase her lingering worries about him. Intellectually, she believed her mother could hold her ground and keep him away, but that's what she would've thought before Randy ever came into their lives. She wasn't afraid for herself, but for her mother and the hell he could put her through just by being around. His relentless harassment of her mother after she filed charges against him had worn on her as much as his abuse had. She had to focus, she couldn't fall apart right here in the post office. "Is Charlie okay?" she asked, numbly realizing Charlie might be hurt.

"He's fine. Dislocated his shoulder, but that's it," Travis said with a glance to Ben.

"Doing good enough to be annoyed he has to wear a sling for a week or so," Ben said.

Once she knew Charlie was okay, Janie latched onto something Ben had said.

"So Darren filed charges against Randy? For what?"

Travis glanced to Ben. "You happen to know that detail?"

"Assault for the incident with his girlfriend and felony assault against an officer," Ben said with a firm nod. "Given his criminal history, he won't be skipping out on bail too easy."

Travis ran his hand through his hair again, his eyes holding Janie's. "Look, no matter what comes of the charges, he won't be getting out anytime soon. There were multiple witnesses for his assault on Charlie, so he won't be able to wiggle out of them."

Janie realized she practically had a death grip on her mail. She eased her grip and tried to marshal the adrenaline pumping through her. Just knowing Randy was in town brought old feelings to the surface—the bitter taste of fear, the wearying sadness of watching her mother be torn down to a sliver of the woman she was, and the slog of getting him out of their lives, both the court case and then his attempts to return afterwards. She realized she was just standing there, staring blankly at the floor when Travis said her name. She looked up and saw nothing but concern and understanding in his eyes. She thought she saw a glimmer of anger, but he blinked it away.

"You okay?" he asked.

"Yeah. I'm fine." She took a gulp of air and looked from him to Ben and back again. "Randy's old news and bad news. I'm glad it sounds like he won't be able to slither out of this one."

Ben caught her eyes. "He's not getting anywhere near you or your mother, so don't even go there."

She managed a nod, feeling exposed to have them both standing here worrying about her. She took care of herself. She always had. She transferred the mail from one hand to the other and shifted on her feet, restless to somehow end this conversation. "I should go. I need to get Stella to recital on time."

"I'll walk out with you," Travis said.

"Catch you later," Ben said generally as they turned away.

Once they were outside, she walked quickly to her car. Travis easily kept pace with her. When she reached her car, she glanced up at him, suddenly awash in the desire to lean into his strength. The snow, which had been coming in fits and starts earlier, was falling in earnest now. He reached for her jacket and gathered it closed, quickly sliding up the zipper. The gesture was so kind and so unexpected, she almost burst into tears. Randy's abrupt return to her orbit had sheered off the walls she'd built around the pain he'd left behind. The hardest part was it wasn't just her pain. If anything, that was the easy part. It was the damage he'd inflicted on her mother—emotionally, mentally and physically.

"You're shivering," Travis said. "Want me to follow you home and take you and Stella to recital practice?"

It surprised her, but she did. It was snowy and blowy, and she was shaky inside. "You don't mind coming back to pick us up?"

"Of course not. Are we allowed to eat in the auditorium?"

"Oh yeah. I do it all the time."

"Perfect. I'll drop you two off and then go grab some takeout."

A warm feeling curled around her heart. He slid his hands from her shoulders down her arms. "Okay, get in your car and drive before you freeze. I'll be right behind you."

CHAPTER 15

*T*ravis juggled a stack of pizza boxes on his way back into the auditorium. Stella had squealed and begged him to get pizza when she heard him mention he planned to pick up takeout while she practiced. Seeing as he couldn't even consider saying no, he'd glanced in the rear view mirror to gauge Janie's reaction. Stella had been riding up front to manage her cast. At Janie's wink, he'd nodded, only to have Stella squeal so loud it hurt his ears.

Once they'd arrived at the recital practice, next thing he'd known, Stella had announced to the entire group that he'd be bringing pizza for everyone. Janie's shoulders had been shaking with quiet laughter when he glanced to her. He didn't mind in the slightest, taking requests before heading out to Glacier Pizza. As he reached the row of seats where Janie was sitting, he could see she was busy reviewing home-work. His heart gave a hard thump. Somehow being here with her sent unfamiliar feelings spiraling through him. It was nothing more than waiting out recital practice and getting pizza for ravenous kids, but he was here with Janie and her presence made the mundane special.

Mrs. Cooper, the music teacher he'd been introduced to before the pizza run, called out for a break. She smiled in his direction when he reached the stage. Before he had a chance to set the pizzas down, he was swarmed.

He simply slid them across the stage and kept a grip on the bottom box, so he and Janie had something to eat. When he made his way down the row to Janie, she glanced up with a grin. "Gotta give it to you. You handled the madness like a champ. Stella can get a tad too excited sometimes, so I hope you don't mind…"

"Of course I don't mind. It's pizza. I love pizza, so it works for me if she loves it too." It crossed his mind that perhaps he should wonder what it meant to be falling so hard and fast for a single mother. Stella was part of the package when it came to Janie, yet not for a second did he blink at that. It helped that he felt an easy affinity with Stella, pizza aside.

Janie shuffled the papers on the tray into a folder and slipped it in her backpack. "Good thing I love pizza too."

With the pizza box balanced on a small tray between two seats, they ate and watched the students circle back to practicing. After Janie declared she was full, he slipped the box out of the way.

"Do you need to keep working?" he asked.

She shrugged. "Not really."

At that moment, the students started on another piece and he turned to watch. He couldn't say he'd ever spent time watching high school students practice for a recital. He was pleasantly surprised to hear how talented they were. Stella was so good at the piano, it was clear a number of the pieces had been chosen to highlight her playing. As time passed, he became hyper-aware of Janie beside him. Somewhere along the way, his hand found its way to rest on her leg. His raw physical attraction to her pulsed inside, and he kept reminding himself this was not the time or place to be thinking the way he felt about her. She glanced sideways, her eyes catching his. Without a word, she curled her hand over his where it rested on her thigh and stood, giving him a swift tug. He'd have followed her anywhere, so that's just what he did.

* * *

JANIE HAD BEEN SITTING beside Travis for what felt like hours, although she knew it hadn't actually been that long. Once the bustle of eating had passed and the students settled back into practice, she lost all ability to focus. Usually she used this time to get caught up on lesson planning and grading. She found it a more efficient use of time than running back and forth to home while Stella practiced. Yet, with Travis here, focusing on anything other than him seemed nearly impossible. Desire swirled within her, its intensity growing with each passing moment. His palm resting on her thigh felt like a hot brand. She was wet with need and restless inside and out.

She suddenly couldn't take it anymore and grabbed his hand, pulling him up with her and striding quickly out of the auditorium. She couldn't explain why, but knowing Randy had somehow made his way back to Diamond Creek set off an emotional bomb inside. She'd have expected to want to wall herself away from Travis, yet the opposite appeared to be happening. She was frantic to feed the fire of her need for him, to lose herself in their scalding connection.

Once they turned down the hallway, she knew just where to go. She didn't teach at the high school, but she knew the layout well. She made a beeline for the office supply closet, practically running by the time she reached the door. She yanked it open and tugged him in behind her. The closet was large with shelves on all four walls. The scent of paper filled the space. A shaft of light fell through a window to the hallway above the door. She spun to face Travis. His features were shadowed, yet his eyes caught the light. Her desire reflected back at her in his gaze.

She still held his hand in hers. He lifted it between them and turned hers over in his, dipping his head to drop a kiss in the center of her palm. The tiny place where his lips connected with her skin sent a shock of sensation rippling outward. One kiss and then pure stillness for a moment before his lips moved to the paper-thin skin on the inside of her wrist, sending slivers of pleasure under the surface of her skin. He lifted his head, the cool air hitting the place where his mouth had left a damp trail. He curled his hand over hers, his thumb caressing the soft skin he'd just kissed.

Her breath was coming in short pants, and she was nearly afire inside and out, heat suffusing her. His back was to the closet door. She held his eyes and placed her palm in the center of his chest. Driven by a wild, pounding need, she stroked boldly down the muscled planes of his chest to curl her palm over the ridge of his cock, hard and hot through the denim of his jeans. His breath drew in with a hiss. She tore at the buttons on his jeans, sighing with delight when she could shove his briefs down far enough to free his shaft. Without waiting, she knelt and dragged her tongue along one side of his cock. He groaned her name and reached for her. She swatted his hands away and knelt down, settling in to drive him as mad as he drove her.

She explored the length of him with her tongue. With a swirl around the thick head of his cock, she took him into her mouth, savoring the subtle salty tang. Between licks, strokes and kisses, she took him into her mouth again and again. She grinned in satisfaction when she pulled back to look up through her lashes. His head was thrown back against the door, his body rigid and his breath coming in sharp, guttural pants. Her pause brought his eyes swinging down to meet hers. He moved so swiftly, she couldn't have stopped him if she wanted. She was lifted and spun around. She almost lost her balance and gripped the edge of one of the shelves as his hands shoved her clothes out of the way. Her shirt was pushed up and with a flick of his thumb, her breasts tumbled loose from her bra.

Her nipples were tight and need clenched her like a vise. She moaned in relief when his warm hands cupped her breasts. He lightly pinched her nipples, just hard enough to make her want more, so much more. His hands slid roughly down her sides, the calloused surface sending hot sparks along her skin. He made quick work of the buttons on her jeans and pushed them down around her hips. Without preamble, he dragged his fingers across the silk of her panties between her thighs and hooked a finger over the edge to delve into her slick channel. She cried out at the feel of his fingers plunging into her. She'd been hovering on the edges of this mad need for him for long enough, she was frantic. Her hips rocked into his hand, and she came quickly in a noisy burst, her cries loud in the small closet.

His touch slowed to a pause before he dragged his fingers out. She glanced over her shoulder to see him tossing his wallet to the floor once he yanked it out of his pocket. She heard the tear of foil and then felt the head of his cock at her entrance. Still throbbing from her climax, all she wanted was to feel him inside of her. Shivers raced up her spine when he slid a palm up the center of her back. With one hand holding her hip firmly, his other brushed her hair off her neck, lacing his fingers into it. He nudged against her entrance, just enough to tease. Barely holding onto her sanity, she arched and pressed her hips into him. He nudged into her a little further.

She threw her head back and arched deeply. He finally surged inside, seating himself fully within her. Her head fell forward, her breath escaping with a low cry at the delicious stretch. They were still again, the air around them electric, before he started to rock into her. In a blur of sensation, they rocked together, her hips pressing back into his again and again and again. She lost herself in nothing but feverish plea-sure. With his hand gripping her hair lightly, she rolled into his surges. Her core drew tight, pleasure twirling inside, until she was hurtling toward another release, the need so deep she could hardly bear it. His hand slipped free of her hip to drag his thumb over her clit. The brush of his touch set her loose again and she cried out, slamming her hips back into his. Her channel convulsed around him as she felt his body go taut with one last surge into her. His guttural cry joined hers.

She slowly came to awareness, slightly amazed to realize she hadn't collapsed. Her hands were gripping the edge of the shelf tightly. The grip of his hand on her hip anchored her. She slowly straightened, and he drew back. In the quiet of the small supply closet, they tugged their clothes back into place. When she saw him glancing around for a trashcan, she snagged a box of tissue from the shelf and tidily wrapped the condom inside before tossing it in the wastebasket in the corner. She turned back to find his eyes on her. In the shadowed light, she felt suddenly vulnerable. This rush of need driving her to him was so unfamiliar she didn't know what to do with it. He seemed to sense she didn't want to talk when she stepped to his side and slipped her hand in his. Once again, she led him through the darkened hallway as they returned to the auditorium.

* * *

TRAVIS STEERED his truck through the darkness, the falling snow sparkling like glitter in the beam of the headlights. Stella was chattering away beside him in the front seat. He couldn't keep his eyes from occasionally looking at Janie in the rear view mirror. He was still half-dazed from their mind-blowing encounter in the office supply closet. If someone had told him he'd fall so hard and fast for a woman, he'd think nothing of screwing her in a closet, he'd have laughed so hard he'd probably have broken a rib. Yet, tonight he was so desperate to have her, it seemed perfectly reasonable. In fact, if he could find another closet right about now, he'd drag her inside and do it all over again.

While Stella talked about a few of the pieces she was practicing and various social dramas, Janie's soft voice sprinkled the conversation. His mind turned his thoughts over in circles. Janie was, well, she was like no other woman. He'd never been the kind of guy to purposefully avoid attachments, but he also hadn't been a player either. He'd been somewhere in between, or so he supposed. He was now discovering the issue had been that he'd yet to meet a woman who called to him on every level. Janie was that woman, and he couldn't quite believe she'd been right under his nose all this time.

He was slightly stunned at the depth of feelings she elicited. Between the slow build between them and Randy's reappearance in Diamond Creek and how it affected Janie, it was beyond clear she meant *a lot* to him. His mind spun back to the look on her face when she realized the call he and Ben had responded to had involved Randy. Just thinking about it now sent a flash of cold anger through him. He'd be perfectly happy to march up to Randy's hospital room and punch his lights out. The only thing holding him back was the knowledge Janie probably wouldn't appreciate the wildfire of gossip that would create, not to mention he'd probably get himself arrested. Though he was friends with everyone on the police force, Darren ran an up and up force. He wouldn't stand for Travis assaulting someone just because of old history.

"Travis?"

Stella's voice snapped him back to where he was. He focused his eyes on the road through the blowing white snow. "Huh?" he asked, glancing sideways at her.

"Oh, I said thanks for the pizza, like three times," she explained with a roll of her eyes. "The rest of the kids liked it too. I was telling Mom you should come to recital practice more often."

He caught Janie's eyes in the rear view mirror at the sound of her muffled laughter. "Anytime," he replied, thinking perhaps they could make good use of the supply closet again.

Janie shook her head with another laugh. "She just wants you to bring more pizza."

Stella laughed and shrugged. "Maybe so, but I like you too." She paused and glanced at Janie before he felt her gaze on him again. He sensed she was considering something. "Okay, you're a guy," she began.

"Yup. I'm a guy," he offered, trying to keep from smiling.

Stella swatted his shoulder. "I have a question. I know what Mom thinks, but I need a guy opinion."

His heart squeezed, a funny warmth spreading through him. It was oddly satisfying to have Stella trust him enough to ask him anything.

"So, did you see the guy who plays the drums?"

At his nod, she continued. "He's my friend, like one of my best friends. I mean, when I first moved here, life sucked. It totally sucked. I didn't know anyone and I was just this loser foster kid from Kenai."

"Stella, please don't..." Janie began.

Stella glanced over her shoulder and threw a smile at Janie. "Mom. I know. You're gonna tell me not to call myself a loser and say something about how words matter. I get it. Don't worry. I don't think I'm a loser now, at least not most of the time. But back then, I did. I'm just trying to explain."

Travis kept driving, figuring it was better to let Stella get to her question at her own pace.

"Anyway, so life sucked. I got to know Parker in music class and he was like one of the only kids who was nice to me at first. Now I have lots more friends, but even though he's a guy, he's like one of my best friends. Okay?"

Travis nodded, thinking she meant for him to confirm he understood. "Got it. Parker's a good guy and he's one of your best friends."

He felt Stella's firm nod. "Right. So anyway, now he's asked me to go to the Christmas Dance. I'm all nervous because I've never been and I'm worried it's weird he asked me and I don't know what it means." Stella's words tripped over each other, coming out in a rush.

His heart clenched again. He couldn't say he knew what it was like to be Stella, but he knew what it was like to be in high school. He was going on twenty years past it, and he was still relieved it was over. He kept his eyes on the road when he sensed Stella felt uncomfortable and strove to keep his tone casual. "So what's your question?"

"Okay, so Mom says it's okay to go to a dance with a friend. But what if it's something else? I don't know why a guy would ask a girl to a dance if he didn't like her as more than a friend. I'm afraid to ask Parker about that because I don't know. So, see—this is why I need a guy opinion. What do you think? Is he just asking as a friend, or is it something more?"

Travis glanced in the rear view mirror. He wished Janie could somehow silently impart some advice here. Her eyes caught his, and one corner of her mouth curled up. She gave a tiny nod that he interpreted to mean it would be okay for him to answer. Although he'd be damned if he knew the right answer. He wished he knew if Stella liked Parker as more than a friend. He sensed she might, but he wasn't sure. After a moment of deliberation, he elected to answer as best he could and pray he didn't unintentionally say the wrong thing.

"Okay, guy answer. Your Mom's right. It's totally okay to go to a dance with a friend. Parker's obviously your friend, so you're cool there. As for whether or not a guy would ask a girl to a dance if he only liked her as a friend, well it depends. I don't know Parker. All I know is he plays drums in music class and recitals with you. He sounds like a pretty nice guy since he was nice to you at a time when it was hard to be the new kid on the block. To make my answer more guy like..." He paused when Stella giggled. "... truth is, most guys ask girls to dances if they like them. So maybe Parker is asking only as a friend, or maybe he's asking a friend who might be hoping there's something more there. Don't go crazy with that answer, but it's my best honest guy guess."

He glanced sideways to see Stella rapidly twirling a lock of hair around her finger. He looked back at the road, slowing to turn off the highway and onto the road that led to Janie's house. Stella sighed. "Fine, so basically it's a big fat maybe. Maybe he just wants to be my friend and maybe he wants something else."

"Yeah, guess so. I bet you wish I could give a guaranteed answer, huh?"

"Yup. That's okay. I'll figure it out."

He turned down Janie's driveway and slowed to a stop. "Are you going to the dance?" he asked as he turned the truck off.

Stella looked over at him before nodding slowly. "It's my senior year. If I don't go this year, I'll never know if I would have had fun or not."

"Damn good reason to go."

Stella's face split in a grin. "Damn right!"

Janie spoke. "Stella, don't start swearing left and right. Okay?"

"Travis swears! You just heard him," Stella countered with a sly grin.

He bit back a chuckle as he unbuckled his seat belt and glanced to Janie with a rueful grin. "Sorry 'bout that."

Janie shook her head with a laugh. "It's okay. I swear too, but Stella has a little too much fun getting going with it."

Stella started to climb out on her own. "Stella! Wait until one of us can help you out," Janie said quickly.

Stella leaned back with an elaborate sigh. "Fine."

Travis got out and quickly jogged around to help Stella. A while later, he found himself leaning on the kitchen counter, sipping hot chocolate Stella had made. She was putting away her homework, while Janie loaded the dishwasher. His eyes were drawn to the glittering lights on the Christmas tree in the living room beyond the stairs. Stella had finished decorating the tree before she started her homework. The home had lights strung festively along the windows and the stair railing. It felt so comfortable to be here, he didn't want to leave, but he figured he needed to find a way to make a graceful exit when Stella looked across the counter at him. "So when are you gonna stop pretending you're not dating my mom and just stay over one night?"

Her sly comment caught Travis off guard and he choked on a sip of hot chocolate. Stella burst out laughing. "I'm not little you know, and I'm definitely not stupid."

He glanced to Janie who closed the dishwasher and put a hand on her hip. "Oh Stella." She laughed softly and shook her head.

Stella shrugged, completely unabashed with her observation. "You're grown ups, so act like it."

At that, she clambered off the stool and grabbed her crutches before heading for the stairs. Travis stared over at Janie whose cheeks were flushed.

CHAPTER 16

*J*anie rubbed her hands together and knocked her boots on the floor, tapping the snow loose. A whoosh of cold air swirled around her as the door to Misty Mountain Café closed behind her. It had been snowing steadily since last night. She'd woken this morning to learn classes were canceled, not because of the snow, but because the boiler broke at the elementary school. Snow didn't stop much of anything in Alaska, but lack of heat did. She glanced around the coffee shop to see if her mother had arrived yet. When she didn't see her, she went to stand in the back of the line. The air was scented with gingerbread and the café decorated with lights and a small Christmas tree on one of the tables. As she waited, her mind spun to last night. Travis had ended up spending the night. Just thinking about it sent a flush over her skin. It felt so good, so damn good, to fall asleep curled up against him. His body was all hard muscle and heat. She was already wondering when she'd see him again, which gave her pause inside. A whopping total of two nights with him and thinking about a night without him almost pained her physically.

She tried to force her thoughts off of him with a look around. Scanning the coffee shop, she saw a few familiar faces. Misty Mountain Café had been around for years and was a local favorite. They served phenomenal coffee and yummy baked goods. Housed in a renovated Quonset hut, the coffee shop made the space warm and homey with artwork on the walls, bright tablecloths and and the ever-present scent of baked goods filling the space. She finally made it to the front of the line and ordered her coffee, along with her mother's favorite. The simple act of ordering coffee made her think of Travis because he'd offered to start coffee this morning when she began the task, and then got sidetracked feeding Pansy and helping Stella get some materials together for a science project.

Her mind flashed forward a little earlier to when she'd woken up. He'd been spooned behind her. She'd felt completely encompassed in his warmth and strength and would have happily stayed there all day. The moment she'd shifted her hips, she'd felt the velvet heat of his shaft against her. "Ignore it," he'd said, his voice gruff with sleep.

Her hips had seemed to have a mind of their own though and arched into him. Next thing she knew, he'd spun her over and kissed her senseless. In several heated moments, so hot and so intense that she blushed right now, he'd mapped her body with his lips and sank inside of her. Her climax had burst through her with such force, she'd been limp in the aftermath. They'd stumbled into the shower, and she'd somehow pulled herself together to walk downstairs as if it were any other day.

Stella was surprising Janie with her frank acceptance of the situation. In the years since she'd fostered and then adopted Stella, she hadn't gone on a single date, so she couldn't have known how Stella would handle it. Watching how Stella looked to Travis for guidance warmed her. Janie's name was called, snapping her out of her brief reverie. She glanced up to find the barista spinning away from the counter after setting two coffees down. After picking them up, she snagged a table by the windows and waited for her mother. Disconcerting though it was, thinking about Travis was more comfortable than thinking about Randy's reappearance in Diamond Creek.

After the haze of passion had worn off and Stella had hitched a ride to school with a friend's mother, Janie had looked to Travis when he was tugging on his coat. "Will you check with Darren for any updates on Randy?" she'd asked.

Those blue eyes of his slammed into hers. He'd simply stepped across the kitchen and curled his strong hands around hers. "Already planned on it. Look, I know we didn't talk about it..."

"It's okay. I'd have guessed you heard about him. Diamond Creek's pretty small, so it's kinda hard to avoid gossip."

His eyes still holding hers, he'd nodded. "Right. Well, I'll check in with Darren as soon as I get to the station. No matter what, I don't think you and your mom need to worry about him this time."

She gave her head a shake, staring out into the falling snow. She didn't like that Randy was like an old thorn burrowed under her skin—one of lingering worry and dull pain. She just wanted to know he couldn't try to push his way back into her mother's life. She swung her eyes up when she heard her mother's voice.

"Hey Mom," Janie said with a small wave, seeing her mother pause near the entrance to greet someone.

Her mother glanced her way and returned the wave. She finished chatting and then headed toward Janie, slipping into the chair across from her.

"Got your coffee already," Janie said as she slid the coffee cup across the table.

"Oh perfect!" Her mother took a sip and sighed. "So good and warm. It's freezing out there today."

"I know. With the wind up and the snow coming down, it looks like we're in for a long, cold day. But it's winter, so I suppose we should expect this," Janie replied with a shrug.

Her mother rolled her eyes. "Of course, but it doesn't mean we can't complain about the cold."

Janie laughed softly and took a swallow of her own coffee, savoring the bitter flavor. She'd steeled herself to get through this conversation, so she eyed her mother and jumped right in. "I wanted to grab coffee with you anyway, but I also had something to discuss."

Her mother arched a brow. "Oh? Are you going to give me the scoop on you and Travis?"

Her mother's question sent a flush to her cheeks. "Maybe, but that's not what I wanted to talk about." It was so tempting, oh so tempting, to let the conversation go in another direction, but she knew if she didn't tell her mother about Randy, she'd hear it from another channel. She took another sip of coffee and steeled herself. "Randy was arrested yesterday," she said flatly.

Her mother's eyes widened and then a familiar expression stole over her face. Janie never forgot the practiced blankness on her mother's face from those years when Randy blotted their life. That's what she saw now—the careful control, the wiping of all emotion. Any expression misinterpreted by Randy could lead to an abusive rant or violence. She swallowed against a flash of anger at seeing the old expression on her mother's face.

She reached across the table and gripped her mother's hand. "Mom, he's in jail. Probably for a long time now."

Her mother's hand, initially still inside hers, squeezed back. "You really think so?"

Janie quickly summarized what she knew of the events leading to Randy's arrest. Her mother nodded along, her eyes widening when Janie mentioned Randy assaulted Charlie. "Oh no! Do you know if Charlie's okay?"

Janie nodded quickly. "He's fine. He dislocated his shoulder, nothing more. Travis was going to check with Darren and let me know any updates." She paused, trying to gauge how her mother was doing. The blank expression had disappeared. For that, Janie was profoundly relieved. Each time Randy had tried to weasel his way back into her mother's life, she'd watched and worried. She'd never doubted her mother didn't want Randy to return and, in fact, resisted it with all of her might. Yet, she knew what he'd been able to do once upon a time—wear her down and strip her defenses away, along with her joy and vitality. The intellectual knowledge of the facts at hand—that Randy had assaulted a police officer with multiple witnesses present—didn't allay her initial worry for how it might affect her mother to learn Randy had once again made his way back to Diamond Creek.

Her mother squeezed Janie's hand firmly. "I'm okay, hon. I was shocked at first because, well, he's been gone for so long." She paused for a sip of coffee. "I wish I could say it surprised me he managed to get arrested again, but it doesn't. Do you know who the woman was?"

Janie shook her head. "No. I was wondering myself. I'm sure Travis can find out."

Leslie shook her head. "No need. I'll probably pay a visit to Darren myself."

The anxiety churning in Janie's gut eased. The shock of the news had passed, and her mother only seemed stronger. "Okay then. Well, keep me posted. You sure you're okay?"

"Hon, I'm fine. I really am. Life is what it is. I was always prepared for him to make his way back here. All he's ever done is bounce back and forth between Fairbanks and Diamond Creek. Stands to reason he'd burn another bridge there and come running. I'm sad to hear he assaulted Charlie, but knowing Charlie's okay means I can be relieved Randy's facing more serious charges for once." Leslie lifted a shoulder in a small shrug. "Only Randy would think assaulting a cop was a good idea." She straightened her shoulders and took another sip of coffee. With a shake of her head, she looked over at Janie. "Enough of that. Let's talk about something else. If there's one thing a few years of therapy taught me, it's not to dwell on things I can't do a damn thing about."

Janie leaned back in her chair and angled her head to the side. "Alright then. Here I was worried about telling you about this."

Leslie eyed her for a long moment. "Of course you were. Randy tore me down so far, I hardly recognized myself. I don't like thinking it, but it was probably worse for you because you had to watch it and worry about both of us all the time. I'm okay. I really am. I just hope you listen to what I told you about Travis. Don't let the past get in the way of a future for you."

Janie rolled her eyes. "Wow, you're slick. You spun right onto Travis."

Leslie's eyes gleamed. "I sure did. So, tell me about Travis."

With a shake of her head, Janie humored her mother's shift in topic. She didn't have much to offer about Travis, especially since she didn't quite feel comfortable sharing details about the churning, burning attraction between them.

* * *

TRAVIS HELD tight to the mooring line and turned his face away from the spray of seawater. It was early afternoon and he'd agreed to help Nathan and his brothers get their larger fishing vessel out of the harbor. Normally, he wouldn't want to be out in the harbor with the snow blowing and wind sending a mist of seawater across the docks. Yet, the reason they were doing this in crappy weather was a leak of unknown origin on the boat. He glanced up toward the boat deck. "Didn't you say you were coming down now?" he called out in Nathan's direction.

Nathan leaned over the railing to reply when his

hat got blown off. The wind caught it, sending the navy blue hat in a somersault before it dropped with a splash into the water. "Dammit! See where my hat went?" Nathan called down.

"In the drink. You'll have to let it go. Maybe you'll be cold enough now to hurry up."

Travis heard Jared's laugh from behind. He glanced back to see Jared approaching on the dock. "Nathan's finally coming off the boat, so you'll be able to let go of that mooring line soon," Jared said with a lift of his chin toward where Nathan was climbing down the ladder onto the dock.

Nathan's feet thumped onto the dock, and Travis released the line holding the boat snug against the dock. Travis glanced back to Jared. "Thought you were meeting us over at the lift?"

"I swapped with Luke. He's waiting at the lift. I'll drive the boat over there."

"Ready to roll," Nathan said when he reached them. He held up a small set of keys.

With the wind gusting and icy snow pelting, Travis helped them get the boat into the lift and out of the water. They got it set on the massive trailer, but collectively decided to wait to move it to the storage facility on another day when the weather was better. A while later, Travis followed Nathan and Jared into Sally's. A hot meal and good drinks were in order after a few hours in the wind and snow. Luke had headed home early. Travis leaned back in the booth and slid the menu to the end of the table.

Their waitress grinned. "No food tonight?" she asked.

"Oh, I'm definitely eating. I just don't need to bother thinking about what I'm getting. I'll take a burger, medium rare. Add a house draft, and I'm good to go."

The waitress held his gaze and nodded as she jotted down his order. Moments later, she spun away after she took orders from Nathan and Jared. Sally's was busy as usual. Inclement weather tended to bring people out of their houses in Alaska, rather than the opposite. Places like Sally's offered the comfort of warmth and good company on those days.

Dinner passed uneventfully as they chatted casually and chowed down. When their waitress left again after bringing coffees to finish off the evening, Jared caught Travis's eyes in his sharp green gaze. "Well, I guess Nathan's right about you."

"Right about what?" Travis asked after a sip of coffee.

"You and Janie. He says…" Jared paused and nodded in Nathan's direction. "…you've finally met your match in Janie."

Discomfited by Jared's apt observation based on nothing as far as Travis could tell, Travis stared back at him. "What makes you say that?"

Nathan chuckled. "Oh, maybe the fact the poor waitress is about to tie herself in knots trying to flirt with you and you're so oblivious, you haven't even noticed. Days past, you might not have gone for it, but you were never one to pass up on a little attention."

Travis was momentarily stunned and then he burst out laughing. "Gotta say, I honestly didn't notice. I'm not so sure how you get from that to Janie…"

It was Jared's turn to chuckle. He took a gulp of coffee and shrugged. "What Nathan said. You're so oblivious, I feel bad for the waitress. If you ask me, it's about damn time you found someone. Take it from a man who used to be committed to being single, it's way better the other way around. Plus, Janie rocks."

Travis took his own gulp of coffee and glanced between Nathan and Jared. At that moment, the waitress in question who'd allegedly been flirting with him returned to their table with the check. When she set it down with a flourish, Travis actually noticed her more than in passing for the first time tonight. She had dark blonde hair tied up in a ponytail high on her head and wide brown eyes. She was tall and leggy, and once upon a time Travis probably would have noticed her. He most certainly would have enjoyed bantering with her because casual banter and flirting was right up his alley. He noticed her gaze lingering on him, her smile focused like a wide ray of light upon him. He managed a smile back, but he seriously didn't feel a thing and wasn't the slightest bit interested. All he wondered was whether or not it was too late to text Janie and stop by her place.

After the waitress wandered off, he looked back over at Nathan and Jared. "So how come she wasn't flirting with you guys?"

Jared rolled his eyes. "Because she knows we're taken. Good grief, when's the last time you happened to come to Sally's? Karen's been working here for months. She's waited on Susie and me a few times. You, however, are another matter, and she clearly knows that. But you look about bored to death, so I'm guessing Janie's it for you."

A while later, Travis walked into his quiet apartment and flicked a light on. Jared's comments had stuck with him. A part of him wanted to shrug them off, but most of him knew they were spot on. After he hung his jacket up and kicked his boots off, he walked into the kitchen and filled a glass of water, draining it quickly. He rinsed it and set it in the drying rack, oddly noting that there were no other dishes cluttering his sink—quite unlike Janie's kitchen, which tended toward clutter, reflecting the comfort of her life with Stella. He fell asleep with the sound of snow pelting against the windows, thoughts of Janie tumbling through his mind.

CHAPTER 17

A week had passed since Travis had spent the night with her with Stella's teasing blessing. In the time since, Janie discovered herself craving every minute of time with him. If she let herself, she might admit she was falling for him. Hard. He hadn't been with her every night, but roughly every other night. She could only imagine how ridiculous she might be if she wasn't a busy single mother. Life didn't allow her to throw everything to the wayside and dive recklessly into a relationship. That detail didn't change the fact that a rather large part of her heart wished she could.

Even more startling was the fact this was happening against the backdrop of Randy's inglorious return to Diamond Creek. A police officer getting assaulted was news anywhere, but it was serious news in Diamond Creek. Randy's bad history around town didn't help matters. As Janie had worried, her mother was inundated with friends and acquaintances asking her how she was doing, if she heard what happened and so on. The last time Randy had made the news in Diamond Creek, it had been for his assault against Janie.

With the buzz going on around Randy, Janie was almost relieved to be so absorbed in Travis. Perhaps if her mother hadn't seemed as rock solid as she did, Janie might've been distracted. Time passed in a blink and next thing Janie knew, Thanksgiving was upon them. Travis was going to Anchorage for the day and night to see his family. Janie hadn't been surprised by his plans, yet a part of her wanted him to be able to share the day with her and her family.

Late in the afternoon before Thanksgiving, she paused in the middle of rolling dough for pies, startled to realize she'd slipped right into a place she'd promised herself she'd never go. In a short span of time, Travis had become a part of her life in more ways than one. It wasn't just the time he spent with her, but the amount of space he took in her heart, mind and body when he wasn't around. In many ways, she could say she was making up for lost time when it came to their searing and body melting sexual encounters. Dear God, the man was uniquely endowed with the ability to make her completely lose her mind. As a woman who'd thought she missed the boat when it came to good sex, Travis was more than making up for her short list of underwhelming encounters before.

Yet, this was what she didn't want. This lingering wish he'd be here for the holiday. This fuzzy, vague hope for a future with him. She didn't think Travis would turn into someone like Randy, but she didn't know if he was falling for her the way she was for him. It was hard to imagine he was. He was too together to get this ridiculous. With a shake, Janie started moving the rolling pin again. She'd find a way to get her wits about her. Whatever happened, she didn't want to make a fool of herself over any man.

* * *

TRAVIS DROVE ALONG THE HIGHWAY, heading south from Anchorage to Diamond Creek. Thanksgiving had been fine, yet he'd missed Janie the whole time. He usually spent the holiday with his parents and a few other relatives in Anchorage. It was always a relaxing, comfortable gathering. Yet, Janie's absence had rung like a bell for him. The only factor holding him back from returning a day early had been a nasty storm through the mountain pass. The Kenai Peninsula, where Diamond Creek was situated roughly halfway down, was south of Anchorage with a mountain range between Anchorage and the peninsula. Travis was generally unbothered by driving through snowstorms, as most Alaskans had to be to get anything done in the winter, however he wasn't stupid. Trying to get through the pass in the snowstorm yesterday evening would've been risky and plain dumb, so he'd stuck to his original plan to return to Diamond Creek the day after Thanksgiving.

As such, he was now damn impatient to get there. He'd texted Janie about stopping by this evening and had yet to hear back. He crested a hill south of Kenai and picked up his speed slightly. The highway that wound its way south on the Kenai Peninsula, Sterling Highway, offered nothing but spectacular views. Cook Inlet, the inlet fed by the Pacific Ocean, was visible almost the entire drive south. Gorgeous vistas of the ocean waters set against the backdrop of the mountains on the far side peeked in and out of view. By the time Travis crested the hill into Diamond Creek, the sun was setting. In Alaska in late November, that meant it was only late afternoon. Diamond Creek came into view where it was nestled into the foothills of the mountains against a blaze of color in the sky—a swirl of pink, red and lavender.

Travis swung by his apartment to drop off his bag, checking his phone once he was in the kitchen. Janie had finally replied to his text, saying it was 'fine' for him to stop by. He raced through a shower to wash the drive off of him and headed over to her house. Stella answered the kitchen door with a wide smile.

"Hey Travis! Come on in. Mom's upstairs changing. She just taught me how to change a flat tire," Stella offered by way of greeting.

Travis returned her grin and followed her inside. Stella was in her usual attire, which landed somewhere between goth and outdoorsy. At the moment, she wore black leggings with a denim skirt over them and a large flannel button-down thrown over a t-shirt. A pair of beat up black leather boots completed her ensemble. As he reached the counter, he suddenly realized her cast was off. "Hey, no cast!"

Stella spun around, another smile splitting her face. "I know! This morning Mom took me in for the first follow up check. Dr. Marshall said I'm all set. I'm supposed to be careful for the next six weeks. No sledding or anything like that. I'm just so happy I won't have to clunk around in my cast for recitals."

Travis snagged a stool by the counter across from Stella. "When is your first recital?"

"Tomorrow. Are you coming?"

"As long as it's okay with your mom."

"As long as what's okay?" Janie asked.

The mere sound of her voice sent a jolt of lust and longing through him. Holy hell. Two days away from her, and he felt like he was lost in the desert, parched for thirst. She was the water he needed. With a mental shake and the clear awareness that Stella was sitting right there as their witness, he spun on his stool to look in Janie's direction. His heart gave a hard thump at the sight of her. Her dark hair, so often tied up and out of the way, fell in damp waves around her shoulders. Her porcelain skin was slightly flushed and her eyes were bright. Lust lashed him like a whip. She elicited an intense combination of feelings—raw lust mixed with an emotional need he'd never experienced. He forced himself to stay where he was. He had to recall what she'd just said. Oh right, Janie's recital.

"Stella wants to know if I'm coming to her recital tomorrow." His voice came out huskier than he intended. He forced himself to breathe slowly in a weak effort to get his body under control.

Janie had paused at the bottom of the stairs. She caught his eyes, and he lost his breath again. The air between them came alive, and she was all the way across the room. For a flash, he sensed a guardedness to her, but the feeling disappeared as quickly as it came. She nodded, a smile curling the corners of her mouth—her delectable, eminently kissable mouth. "Of course! I go to all of them. There's one every week between now and Christmas."

"And two during Christmas week. I think you should come to all of them and bring us pizza after," Stella added with a sly grin.

Travis chuckled in return. He was unaccountably pleased Stella was comfortable enough to joke with him. If he meant to be a part of Janie's life, that included Stella, so he could only hope she'd accept his involvement. Joking around over pizza didn't mean much, but it was something.

Janie walked across the kitchen and opened the oven. As she pulled out a casserole pan of something that smelled amazing, she replied. "You can come to as many as you'd like, but don't let Stella guilt you into buying pizza for them."

Travis glanced to Stella who looked unabashed. "It can't hurt to suggest, right?"

He shook his head with a laugh. "Definitely not. Anyway, I'll be there tomorrow night, and I might get pizza for afterwards."

Janie removed the foil from the casserole pan and got plates out of the cabinet above. "Tonight it's lasagna. Grab a plate," she said with a wave for them to come over.

A few hours later, Travis leaned his head back on the couch with a sigh. He was getting rather comfortable with evenings here. He hadn't spent tons of time around teenagers, yet he found Stella pretty easy to be around. He had enough sense to realize she was likely on her better behavior around him, but she was sly and funny and also content to do her own thing, usually finishing her homework before heading off to her room to play video games and text with friends. Janie had checked on her a few minutes earlier to make sure lights were out.

The television news rumbled in the background and the fire was slowly dying out in the fireplace. Janie was sorting through spelling homework at the moment. Her hair fell forward, catching glints of light from the fire. Without thinking, he let his arm slide off the back of the couch to sift through her hair, brushing it away from her neck and stroking his thumb along the soft skin there.

Her breath hitched and she glanced sideways at him. The air sizzled to life between them. Her eyes locked with his as she slowly angled toward him. The papers in her hand fell to her lap and slipped to the floor in a rustle. She spun to face him, straddling his lap and instantly sending the low hum of need inside into an inferno. He was rock-hard and burning for her the moment she settled her hips down. He'd come to love the way she was—a mix of hesitant and bold. Once any initial shyness wore off, she was abandoned in every kiss and every touch. In a flash, her lips were against his, her hands gripping his hair. He poured himself into their kiss, delving deeply into her hot, sweet mouth while his hands traced her curves. She rocked her hips against him, sending surge upon surge of need scoring through him.

She suddenly tore her lips free. "Upstairs," she said, the single word barely audible.

Travis had to forcefully shake his head to break through the fog of lust clouding his brain. "Why…?" he asked, curling his hands under her breasts to cup them and rolling her hard nipples between his fingers through the thin cotton of her shirt.

She shifted her hips restlessly, sending another hot jolt of need and hardening his cock even more. "Because…" A low moan escaped. "What if Stella comes downstairs? We can't…"

"Right." He finally got it. Only Janie could make him forget her daughter happened to be nearby. He adjusted Janie in his lap and stood with her in his arms. She gave a little squeak and gasp, but curled her legs around his hips. He moved swiftly, striding to the stairs and walking up. With every step, her hips shifted against him. He could feel the damp heat of her through their clothing. He shouldered through the door to her bedroom and had to force himself not to slam it shut, seeing as that could easily awaken Stella.

Without letting her go, he stepped to the bed and turned, sitting down with her in his lap, a bundle of lush curves. He started to kiss her again, but she put a palm on his chest and pushed him back. She reached down with one hand and lifted the hem of her shirt. With a whoosh, it flew over her head and fell to the floor in a rumple. His eyes dipped to see her nipples, taut and peaked, through the black lace of her bra. The dusky pink winked at him through the lace. He didn't wait and leaned forward to swirl his tongue over the lace, growling against her skin when she cried out softly. He alternated between her breasts, drenching the lace with licks, kisses and soft bites. She interrupted him when she yanked at his shirt, tossing it aside where it fell in a heap by hers. The next few moments were a blur. In a tangle of limbs and in between kisses and rough touches, their clothes were torn off. He found himself stretching out beside her, tracing her curves again, this time savoring the feel of her silky skin. He coasted over the soft curve of her abdomen and dipped down between her thighs, almost groaning aloud when she sighed as he dragged a finger through her slick folds.

He rose up on an elbow and trailed his lips behind his touch, pausing to look up at her when he reached the juncture between her thighs. Her head was thrown back against the pillows, her hair a dark tangle around her face and her skin glistening in the dim light. He delved into her channel with one finger and then another. With her hips arching into his slow strokes, he brought his mouth to her. She tasted salty and sweet and nearly drove him mad with the restless roll of her hips and her breathy cries. He settled in to try to drive her as wild as she drove him. Licking, stroking, sucking and plunging his fingers into her drenched channel again and again, he didn't stop until her body went rigid and her channel convulsed around him.

He mapped his way back up her body, leaving a trail of wet kisses across her belly and breasts. In the haze, he managed to remember to snag a condom out of his jeans, which had fallen to the floor, and roll it on. He eased his weight atop her, pausing with his cock resting right at her entrance. He could feel her wet heat against him and had to fight to force himself to slow down, hanging onto a thin thread of control.

"Janie."

Her eyes opened, hazy with passion. He brushed her tangled hair off of her forehead. Her palm slid down his spine, and she curled her legs around his hips. "Travis. Now!" She flexed against him as she spoke, her words rough and demanding.

The thread of his restraint snapped, and he surged into her in one deep stroke, seating himself fully inside of her.

* * *

JANIE HEARD her rough cry as Travis sank inside of her. She was so out of her mind with need, she barely recognized herself. Everything had been whittled down to this moment—nothing but sensation and this incandescent intimacy between them. His gaze was almost navy, darkened with passion. He held still for a long moment, and she felt her body relax around him. She tried to catch her breath, but she couldn't. The moment he started to move, the echoes of her last climax began to spin, building and swirling into another knot of pleasure in her core.

He drove deeply, again and again. His hands curled over hers, and she held on with everything she had. With his hips pounding against hers, she flexed into every stroke as the pressure built inside again. She was losing control and barreled toward another release. His hands gripped hers tightly as tremors began to wrack her body. With a deep surge inside, the wave broke and sharp streaks of pleasure rippled through her. Her channel throbbed around his cock as he went taut as a bow and cried out roughly. She felt the crescendo rise and fall within him before he eased against her, immediately shifting his weight to one side.

The only sound in the room was their rough breathing, slowing in unison. After several long moments, she felt him push up on an elbow and somehow managed to drag her eyes open. When she met his gaze, the moment felt raw and bare, the intimacy so acute, it grabbed ahold of her heart and stole her breath.

anie stood in the audience, cheering along with everyone else as Stella played the final notes in the recital. A gorgeous live spruce tree decorated with lights and red bows provided the backdrop of the scene with lights and spruce wreaths hanging festively throughout the auditorium. Travis was standing at her side. In the years Stella had been playing the piano in school performances, Janie had become accustomed to the rush afterwards. Diamond Creek felt both small and large in these times. Many parents and locals crowded the auditorium, and the space felt enormous. Yet, many of the faces were familiar. It was strange to have someone outside of her family and friends here with her. The cheering gradually died down and people began to gather their jackets and file out of the rows of seats.

Janie's mother stood on one side of her with Travis to the other. Leslie nudged Janie's elbow. "Are we going backstage?"

Janie glanced to her. "Of course. Let's give it a few minutes though. It's a bit of a madhouse at first." She plunked down in her seat, only to glance up at the sound of her name.

Tess and Nathan were weaving their way through the aisle. "Hey!" Tess said with a wave when she reached the end of their row.

"Hey, didn't know you two would be here tonight," Travis commented.

Nathan flashed a roguish grin. "Of course. With Tess's business, you know we don't miss a single one of these."

Tess ran a fundraising and event coordinating business, which covered most of Southcentral Alaska. She was routinely responsible for helping coordinate various local events, including the run of holiday recitals for the high school. Tess elbowed him in the side with a roll of her eyes. "That's not the only reason we come. I wanted to be here tonight to see the first performance," she said with a smile at Janie. Her eyes flicked to Travis and back, a subtle gleam entering her gaze.

Janie's mother smiled proudly. "Stella was amazing, as always. If you ask me, she's the star of every performance."

Tess grinned. "Of course she is!"

A family friend approached and the conversation expanded. A little while later, Janie was standing with a hip hitched on the back of one of the seats while Nathan and Travis talked fishing. Tess was at her side and leaned down. "In case you were wondering, Travis can hardly keep his eyes off of you," she said in a low voice.

Janie glanced to her, a flush spreading up her neck

and face. She shook her head the tiniest bit. "You can't help but tease."

Tess's expression sobered. "You're my friend, and it's nice to see you happy. Even better, nice to see a guy drooling over you the way you should be drooled over."

Janie blushed a little harder and rolled her eyes, disconcerted to think any man noticed her that way. "Okay, enough."

A while later, the group slowly broke apart and Janie, Travis and her mother made their way backstage. When they entered the area, Janie saw a stack of pizza boxes on the table against the back wall. She looked up at Travis. "Did you…?"

He nodded. "Yup, had it delivered. Don't worry, I won't get them pizza after every recital, but since this was their first performance, I thought they deserved it."

Her mother burst out laughing. "They'll love it no matter what!" She squeezed his arm. "I like you, Travis."

Janie's heart did a little somersault and flutters twirled through her belly. She was starting to worry her feelings for Travis might be a lot more than like. His arm was draped over her shoulders, the heat of it comforting and distracting at once. With her pulse racing, she took a breath and glanced around. In addition to the pizza, someone else had brought platters of holiday cookies and mulled cider, the scent filling the air and carrying the holiday feeling from the recital backstage. At that moment, Stella walked over to them, a piece of pizza in her hand. "Thanks Travis!" She bounced to his side and gave him a half-hug with her free arm.

A while later, they walked outside of the school into the cold night. The air was sharp, bordering on brutally cold. Stella was still chattering almost non-stop. She was always like this after a performance, high on adrenaline and buzzing with energy. They rode home in Travis's truck. While Stella talked and Travis gamely humored her, Janie was quiet as she watched the nightly landscape. The moon was close to full, its light casting a glow across the bay and onto the snowy ground. The stars were bright against the velvety sky.

Janie fell asleep with Travis beside her after he sent her body and mind hurtling through intense pleasure. She woke early the following morning. Bright sun fell through the window across the bed. She was getting used to waking with him. She loved the feel of his muscled body beside hers and the heat he emanated. Even in sleep, he exuded pure masculinity. She traced the hard planes of his chest with her fingertip and wondered how to gain a foothold on her sanity again. Because what she wanted was starting to frighten her. She wanted all kinds of things she'd never let herself hope for—nights like last night every night, the comfort of knowing Travis would be here always. She couldn't lose herself in this. She was no longer afraid Travis would suddenly show her a different side of himself. That she didn't doubt. Yet, years of carefully guarding her heart and making sure she didn't hope for anything had created a powerful narrative in her mind—one that didn't include allowing herself to be vulnerable to any man. She'd thrived within the independent life she'd created for herself, a life where she felt fulfilled, enjoyed being able to rely on herself and nurtured her relationships with family and friends. It had never felt like less than anything, and still didn't. Yet now, Travis took up so much space in her heart, body and mind that it worried her.

Later that afternoon, Janie was busy cleaning. It was Saturday, and she was doing what she usually did on Saturday—chores. Unsettled with how comfortable she was getting with Travis, she'd brushed him off this morning and insisted she had other things to do when he offered to take her and Stella out for breakfast. Stella had sulked briefly about it, but she'd quickly moved on to texting back and forth with friends. After cleaning the house, Janie tossed the trash and recycling in the back of her car and headed off to swing by the dump. She stopped her car at the top of the hill on the way out of the dump's parking lot. Only in Alaska could someone consider going to the dump a scenic trip. Eagles were posted on every tree and any other possible resting spot. They swarmed the dump for scraps on most afternoons. Her eyes landed on an eagle stationed atop a boulder at the base of the drive into the parking lot. The eagle turned its head slowly, its sharp eyes landing on her. The regal bird quickly decided she wasn't worth staring at and turned its head away again.

She looked beyond the highway to Kachemak Bay. Wind gusted forcefully today leaving the surface of the water choppy. The mountains on the far side of the bay were topped with snow, offering a stunning view of the jagged peaks against the bright blue sky. Looking out over this familiar view called to her heart because it was home. It settled her inside. Her gut had been churning with anxiety since last night. She needed to re-establish some sense of internal control when it came to Travis. At this moment, she felt calm and rational. She'd back off and slow things down. It was what she needed, and it was the smart thing to do for Stella. She didn't want to barrel into this relationship with Travis without considering Stella. Stella was already getting attached to him, and Janie didn't even know where things might be going with him, or how he might feel about any of it, including her ready-made family.

* * *

TRAVIS KICKED the snow off of his boots and stepped through the main entrance to the fire station. He quickly grabbed the shovel tucked by the door and stepped back outside. Within seconds, he'd cleared the snow that had already started to pile up in front of the door. A fast-moving snowstorm had rolled in last night, and they were still in the thick of it. He made his way back inside and aimed straight for the break room, pulling his phone out to check it out of habit. It had been almost a week since he'd had a night with Janie, and he was about half-crazed because of it. It wasn't that she wasn't talking to him, it was that she dodged every attempt he made to try to see her. He'd texted this morning before he left to see if he could stop by tonight. As of yet, no reply from her.

He walked into the break room and strode right to the coffee pot. He didn't even look and started to lift it when he realized it was empty. "Dammit!" he exclaimed to no one. With a sigh, he set the coffee pot down and started to get another batch ready.

"Dammit what?"

Travis glanced over his shoulder to see Sylvia

entering the room from the other side. "No coffee. You spoil us, so when it's empty, well... you know how I feel," he said with a wry smile.

Sylvia reached his side and nudged him out of the way. "Sit down. I'll get this."

Travis didn't argue and sat down at the table nearby. Sylvia quickly started the coffee and then sat down across from him. She was quiet, although her mere presence was comforting. Sylvia functioned as a quasi-mother to all of them in the station. As such, with him feeling off kilter at the depth of his feelings for Janie and her recent dodges of him, he could use a dose of Sylvia's warm, motherly presence. He ran a hand through his hair with a sigh. Sylvia stood and tugged the coffee pot out, quickly pouring him a cup before putting it back to allow the pot to finish filling. She slid it across the table to him as she sat down again.

"Figured you could use the strongest bit. Cream is right there," she said with a nod to the small container in the center of the table.

He quickly poured a dash of cream in his coffee and took a gulp. Sylvia angled her head to the side. "You don't look too good. Are you okay?"

He considered her question. He didn't know how to answer because everything he was feeling inside was entirely foreign to him. Up to now, when he was having a rough day, it was usually based on the mundane annoyances life tossed out. In many ways, he'd led a charmed life. Beyond his family and close friends, no one had gotten close enough to him to rattle him in this way. As a firefighter and emergency responder, he'd witnessed his share of tragedy and loss, yet those tragedies and losses had belonged to others. He'd witnessed the emotional tidal waves that rocked lives, but he'd never really experienced them for himself. He wasn't equating a week's avoidance from Janie as anything like an actual tragedy, yet his emotional unsteadiness was so startling, he didn't know how to deal with it. He missed her acutely and realized for the first time what it meant to care this deeply for her.

He took another gulp of coffee and met Sylvia's eyes, lifting a shoulder in a half shrug. "Depends on what you mean by okay."

Sylvia stared over at him, her eyes considering. She sighed and leaned back in her chair. "This must have something to do with Janie."

Travis ran a hand through his hair and nodded. "Bingo. This is all new for me. I'm all out of whack and it's just because I haven't seen her in a week. It's nothing major, but she's always got a reason she's busy. I feel stupid saying it out loud, but..." He gulped down more coffee and stood to refill his cup.

"You're not stupid, you're in love," Sylvia said plainly.

He almost dropped his coffee, tightening his fingers around the cup at the last second before it fell loose from his grip. He turned the idea of love over in his mind. Problem was, his mind didn't help much, not when his heart gave a resounding kick at the mention of the word. He returned to the table, unsettled inside. He met Sylvia's warm gaze, his heart pounding rapidly in his chest. "You think?" he finally managed to ask.

Sylvia smiled slightly, nodding slowly as she did. "Oh yes. If she were just a woman you were dating, this wouldn't bother you in the least. You might wonder, but you'd carry on. You certainly wouldn't be moping about the station, cranky and snapping at the slightest thing. You're an easy-going guy and you've been blessed with a life that made you that way. That's why it makes it hard for you to be so stirred up inside. You're not asking my advice, but I'll give it to you. If she's brushing you off, be direct with her. My guess is Janie's as thrown by this as you are."

"You think so?" He didn't want to hope Janie was as unsettled as he was, but it was a relief to think she could be. It might signify she felt something akin to what he did.

"I've known Janie her whole life. Like I told you before, watching what her mother went through with Randy did a number on her. No matter what, this will throw her as much as you."

Travis's radio crackled from where he'd tossed it on the table. A report came through about a fire up on the hillside. He stood quickly and guzzled his coffee. "Gotta go!"

As he reached the door, he glanced back. "Thanks for the advice," he said.

"Always. Make sure you take it!" Her words reached him as he raced down the hall.

Many hours later, he pulled into Janie's driveway. He'd called her on his way back from the fire. It had been yet another chimney fire. Early winter resulted in frequent chimney fires, more often than not caused solely by people choosing not to bother with cleaning their chimney. Janie had started to demur when he asked about stopping by, but he'd taken Sylvia's words to heart, so he'd been direct and told her he wanted to talk. He rolled to a stop and turned the engine off. The snow had ended a few hours ago, leaving several feet of white fluff covering the landscape. He leaned his head back and gathered himself. He hadn't a clue what to say, but he knew he couldn't stand to keep waiting without making sure she knew how he felt. He'd had hours to think since his brief conversation with Sylvia. After they'd dealt with the fire, he'd helped clean the fire trucks back at the station, restless to do anything to keep himself occupied. The activity had kept him busy, but his mind hadn't stopped churning with thoughts of Janie. He was struggling to contain the emotions barreling through him, yet he was certain Sylvia was right. He loved Janie. Now, he just had to find the courage to tell her.

He shook himself and stepped out of the truck. The packed snow crunched under his boots. When he stepped onto the side porch, the kitchen door opened and Pansy dashed past him into the yard, immediately bounding into the snow. Stella stood in the doorway, grinning as she watched Pansy run in mad circles through the snow.

"Hey there," he said.

Stella glanced to him. "Hey! I figured you were here. Pansy got all excited about something. Come on in." She stepped through the door onto the deck and gestured inside.

Travis walked into the kitchen to find Janie putting dishes in the dishwasher. He distantly heard Stella calling Pansy's name. One week. One single week since he'd seen Janie, and it was all he could do not to step to her, lift her in his arms and carry her to the closest place he could find. It wasn't simply the driving need to be with her physically, but the deep need to connect with her intimately. Pansy dashed by him and came to a sliding stop in the middle of the kitchen. She stopped and shook, sending snowflakes in a swirl around her.

Stella closed the door, cold air whooshing in behind her. As she started to skip across the kitchen, Janie closed the dishwasher and looked up. "Stella, take it easy. Your ankle's better, but don't overdo it."

Stella wrinkled her nose and rolled her eyes, but she obediently slowed to a walk and plunked down on a stool by the counter. Janie had yet to address him directly, but conversation carried on with Stella chattering blithely. At some point, she got distracted by a text and meandered out of the kitchen, texting back and forth with Parker. Travis glanced to Janie. "I guess texting is the modern version of talking on the phone for kids, huh?"

Janie burst out laughing. "Absolutely! She almost never makes calls to her friends."

He couldn't help but smile, it was so good to hear her laugh. As they stood there, her smile faded and she looked over at him. "You said you wanted to talk," she finally said.

His chest tightened, and his heart jumpstarted. He managed to nod. "I did. Can I ask you something first?"

She was holding a dishtowel and began to twist it between her hands. After a moment, she nodded.

He didn't have much of a plan for how to have this conversation, and he was definitely navigating uncharted waters, seeing as no woman had ever mattered this much to him. He took a gulp of air. "Have you been avoiding me?" he finally asked.

Her eyes widened, and the towel slid in a loop between her hands. She closed her eyes and took a deep breath before shrugging. "Not on purpose, but maybe that's what ended up happening," she finally said.

Her words were a glancing blow. For a second, he reacted to the idea she was avoiding him, but then he managed to absorb the first part—that she hadn't been avoiding him on purpose. He held onto that.

"Okay. I, uh… Look, I don't know how the hell to explain any of this. It seemed like you were avoiding me, and well, I, uh, I miss seeing you. I guess we haven't talked about us and maybe I should've said something sooner, but this is all new to me, so I didn't. Here's the thing…" He paused to catch his breath when he realized his words were tumbling out in a jumble. When he looked over at Janie to gauge her response, her eyes were pinned to him. He couldn't read her expression. For a split second, he almost decided to forget it. He mentally gave a hard shake and forged ahead. "The thing is I think I love you." That was it. That was all he could say. With his heart hammering, he gulped in air.

The words dropped like a stone in the room. Janie's mouth opened and closed. Her eyes widened again and her breath drew in sharply. The long silence wasn't exactly encouraging. He couldn't say what he expected because he hadn't thought about expecting anything. He'd simply wanted to make sure she knew how he felt.

The towel was twisting in a rapid loop between her hands. She finally spoke. "I…I don't know what to say. I never…" She paused and shook her head sharply. "This is a lot, this thing with us. I won't say I was consciously avoiding you, but I just needed a little time to try to think straight. You see, I don't really do this kind of thing." She dropped the towel from one hand and gestured between them. "I don't know how I feel because I feel half-crazy inside. Can you give me a little time to slow down?"

Travis started across the kitchen. Maybe six feet separated him from Janie, and he fought the urge to close the distance and kiss her. He needed to show her what he meant. He knew what he felt when they were together. Maybe she didn't know if she loved him, but he knew she felt something and something powerful, or it wouldn't feel as if they were bound together by invisible threads. He forced himself to take a deep breath. Disappointment was nearly crushing him. Footsteps sounded in the hallway upstairs, reminding him Stella was here. In another second, she was jogging down the stairs.

"Mom, Parker wants to drive me to the dance next weekend? Is that okay?" Stella slid across the hardwood floor in her socks, skidding to a slow stop beside Janie.

Janie looked to her, her expression blank for a moment. Her eyes came into focus and she started to nod and then paused. "As long as the weather's not bad. I don't want him driving you two around if the roads are slick."

"Mom, but…"

Janie shook her head firmly. "That's the deal. If the weather's bad, his mom and I can decide between us who'll do the driving."

Stella cast her eyes in Travis's direction, but he whole-heartedly agreed with Janie. Not to mention, he wasn't about to put himself at odds in this situation. He shook his head and gestured to Janie. "Don't look at me. I completely agree with your mom."

Stella rolled her eyes and quickly began texting

something on her phone as she walked over to the couch in the living room and plopped down. She snagged the remote and turned the television on. Travis looked to Janie who had returned to twisting the dishtowel in her hands. Much as he wanted to insist she see to reason, or more accurately to heart, now wasn't the time with Stella as an audience. "Look, I'll get outta here. If you wanna talk some more, let me know."

Something flashed in her eyes. "Travis, I didn't mean…"

"It's okay. Now's not the time. You know how I feel. Unless I hear from you, I'll give you the space you're asking for." At that, he tore his eyes away from hers and turned to the door. He was relieved for the low hum from the television, keeping Stella's attention off of them. When he reached the door, he called a good bye to Stella and quickly left, not trusting himself to look in Janie's direction again.

His heart was pounding so hard, he thought he might break a rib. As he drove away, he felt crushed. He didn't know what he'd hoped for, but he'd definitely hoped for a little more than that from Janie. He supposed it was better that she knew how he felt, no matter what it meant for her.

CHAPTER 19

$\mathcal{J}$anie walked down the hallway to her classroom. She'd woken to another gray day, which suited her mood perfectly. Almost a week had passed since Travis stopped by and announced he thought he loved her. In the intervening time, she felt torn to pieces. The truth was, she was pretty sure she loved him too. But she felt like a fool for how she'd reacted when he told her how he felt and one thing after another kept getting in the way of her finding a time to talk with him. Stella had recital practice every night right now, along with the weekly performances themselves. This time of year was always busy at school with students ramping up for testing and the interruptions of the holidays making mischief in the classroom, especially for students who needed routine almost as much as they needed air and water. Her days were filled with managing tiny behavioral outbursts, teaching to tests and racing home to take Stella to practice.

In the meantime, the gossip mill was abuzz over

Randy's return to Diamond Creek and his arrest. It seemed like every time Janie turned around, someone was breathlessly asking her what she thought about it. Over and over, she was reminded of his outsized presence in her mother's history and her own encounter with his fist. His presence was a painful reminder of why she'd chosen a life of independence.

A child raced past her, reaching the door to her classroom seconds before she did. "Danny! Slow down," she called.

Danny skidded to an abrupt stop, his brown hair bouncing comically as he did. He looked up at her when she reached his side. "I didn't wanna be late."

She ruffled his hair. "I'd rather you be a few seconds late than running."

He managed to speed walk to his desk and plop down just as the bell rang. Her day passed in a blur, while most of the time she had trouble focusing. She kept replaying the scene in the kitchen with Travis. By the end of the day, she was frazzled. After the last bell rang and her students hurried out of the classroom, she savored the quiet as she did a quick check of the classroom, tidying a few areas. She'd returned to her desk and was gathering some papers when she heard her name. She glanced up to see Tess walking through the door.

"Hey, what brings you here?" she asked, inordinately pleased to see Tess. She could use a few minutes of Tess's warmth.

Tess brushed a loose curl out of her eyes and shimmied her hips onto Janie's desk. "Checking in with Nancy about the numbers from the last school fundraiser. Figured you might be around, so I thought I'd check. How's it going?"

Janie shrugged. "You know. Busy here, busy at home. Just busy. You?"

"My own kind of busy. This time of year is probably the craziest for me with all the holiday fundraisers. I'll be in Anchorage all weekend for three different events. Nathan's being a good sport and going with me. You know how much he loves wearing a jacket and tie, so…" Tess chuckled.

Janie managed a grin in reply, but it was weak and she knew it. Tess's eyes narrowed. "Are you okay?"

Janie tried to smile again and play it off, but she just didn't have it. She set the papers in her hand down and leaned back in her chair. "I'm tired. I'm sick of people asking me about my mom's ex because all it does is make me remember how shitty things were. So there's that. Oh, and Travis told me he loved me and I forgot how to talk, so we haven't talked in a week."

Tess looked over at her from her perch on the desk, her eyes warm and understanding. "Oh hon. Where should I start?"

Janie's throat was tight and tears were hot against her eyelids. She swallowed against the tightness and took a deep breath. "Uh, wherever you think."

Tess was quiet, her eyes considering. "Well, let's get Randy out of the way first. It's never fun to have to face the past when you can't do a damn thing about it, especially when the hell he put you and your mom through wasn't your fault. All I can say is try to move on. He assaulted a cop, so it's news, but the only way you can stay sane is to try to let it go. My guess is it's bothering you more than it might because of Travis. You made some choices about how you lived your life because of Randy. Travis is calling those choices into question."

Janie stared at Tess, her stomach doing a funny flip. She didn't like to think she was allowing Randy to affect her that much. Tess's eyes were warm and steady as she looked back at Janie. Janie finally took a deep breath, letting it out in a sigh. "Maybe so, but what do I do about it?"

Tess shrugged. "I'm no expert, but with that kind of thing, just acknowledging it goes a long way. You can't change the past, but you can take a hard look at how it's affecting your present and try to make sure you don't let it run your life."

Janie absorbed Tess's words and felt some of the tension bundled up in knots ease slightly. After she nodded slowly, Tess moved on. She was nothing if not efficient in everything she did. "Now, onto Travis. What do you mean you forgot how to talk?"

Janie shrugged, feeling a blush heat her cheeks. She felt like an idiot. She was thirty-three years old and should have some kind of clue how to have a relationship conversation, but she was stumbling along blindly. "Just that. He wanted to talk and said he thought he loved me, and I just couldn't figure out what to say. I did say I wanted some time to slow down, but I think I hurt his feelings. I didn't mean to! He startled me. Stella was home and I just froze. Next thing I knew, he said unless he heard from me, he'd leave me alone. Or something like that."

"How long ago was this?"

"A week."

Tess pursed her lips and cocked her head to the side. "A week and you haven't tried to communicate at all? Text, call, anything?"

Janie threw her hands up and shook her head. "No! What do I say? I'm terrible at this because I have no practice. He freaked me out. I just wanted a little room to breathe and he shows up and says he loves me."

Tess arched a brow. "I think you know exactly how you feel."

"How can you know if I don't know?" Janie asked mulishly.

"If you didn't love him, you wouldn't be worried. You'd be thinking it was all a little awkward, but you'd find a graceful way out. Instead you're frozen. You know what they say about fear?"

"What?" Janie asked with a roll of her eyes. Inside, she was spinning at Tess's blunt observation.

"When people are faced with something they fear, they have three possible ways to react: fight, flight, or freeze. You're freezing. If you weren't afraid, there'd be nothing to freeze up about."

"Oh." Janie's one word response belied how she felt inside—a wild tumble of emotion. Tess's observation was so apt, it frightened her.

"Oh is right," Tess said wryly. "The next question is what do you plan to do about it?"

"That's the problem! I don't know what to do."

"I think you want to talk to him and you're afraid. I get it. I really do. But if you don't want to blow your chance, you might want to stop waiting around."

Janie's heart started beating rapidly at the mere idea of losing this chance with Travis. She stared at Tess, seeing the warmth behind her blunt words in her eyes. She nodded slowly. "Right. Okay. I'll figure this out." She glanced at the clock above the door. "Unfortunately, I'm about to be late to go get Stella to practice." She stood and grabbed her jacket and purse. Tess walked quickly down the hallway with her. When they started to part ways in the parking lot with a cold winter wind gusting, Tess called her name. Janie looked back, her hair blowing wildly in the wind. "What?"

"Don't wait too long. You've got a phone. Use it!"

At that, Tess turned and climbed into her car. Janie stood where she was and watched Tess drive away. She spun around to face the bay. Her eyes were watering from the cold wind, but it felt good. It numbed her outside and in.

* * *

THE FOLLOWING AFTERNOON, Janie watched her students get up in unison at the sound of the bell and race out of her classroom. She sat down with a sigh. After Tess's blunt talk with her yesterday, she'd meant to text Travis last night. Instead, Stella had a mini-meltdown over some girl in her class who she thought liked Parker. Janie had spent the late evening after recital practice listening to Stella rant and trying to help her see what was painfully obvious—that she liked Parker as much more than a friend. Stella had grudgingly admitted that she'd never cared before about girls who liked Parker, but now it mattered 'a lot a lot' to her.

This morning, the guy who plowed her driveway had called to report he'd be late because one of the hinges on the plow needed to be repaired. Janie had shoveled a barely wide enough path to get out of the driveway and make it to work on time after another snowstorm dumped a good foot of snow the night before. She'd been exhausted before class even began. Once again, her mind spun to Travis. The farther away she got from Tess's talk, the more she started to freeze up again. She pulled her phone out of her pocket and considered texting Travis now. But she reasoned she was too tired to be sensible tonight, so she didn't.

CHAPTER 20

*H*ours later, she turned on the late night news. Another evening of reviewing homework and prepping lesson plans during recital practice, and she was finally done with her day. She'd been beyond relieved to discover her circular driveway plowed when she got home. After a quick dinner of leftovers, Stella had dragged herself to bed with Pansy right on her heels. Stella had been as tired as Janie, although her mood had been better after Parker told her he didn't like the girl flirting with him at school. Janie was barely paying attention to the news when she heard Diamond Creek mentioned. She grabbed the remote and turned it up.

"Crews are responding to a massive fire at the Midnight Sun Lodges, a hotel in Diamond Creek. The hotel is one of the largest in the area with over three hundred rooms. Reports from the scene indicate the fire escalated quickly, although we don't yet know the cause. At this point, they've requested support from nearby towns with the Kenai and Homer crews already on the scene. We're told that there were guests present in the hotel, and crews have already confirmed the building was evacuated safely. At the moment, two firefighters are unaccounted for, and we're waiting for an update on their status. We'll report back when we have more information."

Janie could hardly breathe and remained frozen where she was for a moment. Suddenly, she leapt up from the couch, her gut churning and anxiety roiling her. She had to find out if Travis was okay. She didn't doubt for a second he was there. She could only pray he was safe. She started to race upstairs, only to stop when Stella almost ran right into her as she barreled down the stairs. "Mom! We have to go to the harbor. Parker just texted me there's a big fire at Midnight Sky. We have to make sure Travis is okay."

Janie stared up at Stella where she stood a few stairs above her. She'd been meaning to call up to Stella that she would be back in a bit, but Stella's suggestion hit her like a bucket of cold water. She couldn't bring Stella with her. If Travis wasn't okay, if something happened to him, she couldn't let Stella find out that way. As if she could read Janie's mind, Stella shook her head and walked past her on the stairs. "You're not making me wait here. I can bet you're worried how I might react if something happens to him. You forget what I've already gone through. My first mom died of an overdose, and I'm the one who found her. I can deal with all kinds of things. I'm going with you."

Stella practically stomped to the kitchen door and started to pull on her boots. When she straightened up and looked over at Janie, her chin was set and her eyes determined. Janie stared back at her, slightly stunned at Stella's courage. Her chest tightened with emotion to realize how much Stella cared about Travis. Regardless of her concerns about bringing Stella with her, Stella had just made the decision for her. "Okay. You can come with me, but you're staying out of the way. Are we clear?"

Stella nodded quickly. Pansy had followed Stella downstairs and was lingering at her side, her eyes bouncing between Janie and Stella. Stella looked down at her and back to Janie. "We can't take her with us," Janie said firmly.

Stella seemed to realize she'd won her own small battle already, so she nodded. "Okay." She leaned over and stroked Pansy's sleek black head. "We'll be back, Pansy." She straightened again and snagged her coat off its hook on the wall.

After Janie stepped into her boots and tugged her coat on, they walked outside into the icy cold night. Janie was swinging between frantic worry and trying to cling to some sense of holding it together. She didn't want to fall apart in front of Stella, but her fears for Travis were real and close to overwhelming. Stella was quiet on the ride toward Otter Cove Harbor. Midnight Sun Lodges was situated beside the harbor. Janie was a bundle of nerves with anxiety, worry and fear chasing each other in circles inside. Her muscles were taut and she felt sick to the point of verging on nausea. All she could think about was Travis and making sure he was okay.

When they approached the harbor, Janie could see far more lights than usual lighting up the area. As she scanned the parking lot by the hotel, she could see spotlights shining brightly from several fire trucks. Flames were shooting up into the night sky over one wing of the hotel with smoke billowing out and filling the area with haze. There were fire trucks from the Diamond Creek station, along with a few others from Kenai and Homer. Police vehicles were everywhere. A large cluster of people was gathered to one side of the parking lot. Janie guessed that to be everyone who'd been evacuated from the hotel. She parked at a distance and looked over at Stella. "I want you to wait here."

Stella opened her mouth and then closed it promptly. "Fine. Promise you'll come tell me once you know what's going on."

"Promise." Janie checked the heat and left the car running when she climbed out. Stella had already slipped her phone out of her pocket and started to text. Janie figured she was texting back and forth with Parker and some of her friends.

The scent of smoke filled the air. Her boots crunched against the packed snow as she walked toward what appeared to be a makeshift command area with the police chief, Darren, busy chatting with a few officers. All firefighters in sight were manning hoses from the fire trucks and moving in and out of the building. Janie paused and scanned the area, trying to see if she could locate Travis in the milieu. When she couldn't, she lost her breath again for a moment, the fear clogging her throat and chest. She had to force herself to take a slow breath. She strode quickly toward Darren, blinking against the bright lights as she got closer.

Darren was busy looking at a set of plans spread out on a folding table with the Diamond Creek fire chief, Ken Hanson, at his side. When Janie reached them, she saw they were looking at what must be the building plans for the hotel. Darren glanced up to see her. The moment his eyes landed on her, she knew Travis was one of the firefighters missing somewhere in the hotel.

"Where's Travis?" she asked bluntly.

Ken's head whipped up, and Darren glanced to him and back to her. Of the two, she knew Darren better, mostly because he was married to Risa who she'd met through her friendship with Tess. Darren straightened his shoulders. "Hey Janie, right now we're trying to narrow down where he might be. He and Ben were the first ones in the building to help get everyone evacuated. We have a last confirmed location for both of them. Travis was last seen by the stairwell on the third floor. Ben was on the second floor on the other end of the building."

The fear coiling inside of her knotted tighter. She was relieved Darren hadn't bothered to hide the fact Travis was one of the two missing somewhere in the building. She couldn't seem to speak over the rushing sound in her ears. Ken's voice cut through. "We'll find them both, Janie. We've got two crews working to manage the fire and we've sent in pairs to search for them."

She felt herself nodding, but she still couldn't talk. She looked beyond them to the hotel. It had three main wings and was three stories high. It seemed massive to her right now. Travis could be anywhere in there. The possibilities for something bringing harm to him felt endless. All it would take was one of those possibilities. Emotion welled inside, and her knees almost buckled. She felt someone's arm ease around her waist. "Let's get you sitting down," a voice said. Whoever it was moved her a few steps away and helped her sit down in a folding chair. She was too stunned to realize who it was until she managed to gulp in a breath of cold, smoky air. She glanced up to see Sylvia Cunningham resting her hips on the edge of the table.

Sylvia's warm eyes caught hers. "Sit tight. I'll wait with you," she said firmly.

Janie felt strangely numb. The cold didn't bother her in the slightest. She glanced around and felt like she was in the eye of a hurricane with activity swirling around her while she just sat there. She gave herself a shake and looked over at Sylvia. "Shouldn't you be back at the station?"

"I'm not on duty tonight at the 911 line. Michael still keeps his scanner on because the man doesn't seem to understand the meaning of retirement," she began, referencing her husband who used to be the police chief. "When we heard this call come over the scanner, we came down right away. I figured they could use a hand on this side of things. Michael's over there," she said, gesturing to her husband who stood by one of the ambulances.

"Aren't you worried about Travis and Ben?" Janie asked, fighting a rising sense of irritation at Sylvia's calmness and that of Darren and Ken as well.

"Of course! But we can't go letting that drive what we do, can we? You can't do emergency work and lose it every time something might've gone wrong. I'm hoping for the best. These guys know what they're doing. If Travis happened to be out here and one of his buddies was lost in there, he'd be calm and cool because that's what he'd have to be."

Sylvia leaned forward and gripped Janie's hands between hers. "Hold on. Don't go thinking the worst."

Janie realized how icy cold her hands were when Sylvia gave her hands a squeeze before she leaned back again. Janie fumbled in her coat pocket and pulled out a pair of gloves. It was only then she realized she hadn't even bothered to change before they left. She'd stripped out of her work clothes after dinner and tossed on her favorite sweatpants and a t-shirt she usually slept in. She looked over at Sylvia with a shrug as she pulled her gloves on. "I forgot to change before we came down here." She took a deep breath to try to ease the fear racing through her. "I didn't mean to snap at you. I'm usually calm, even in emergencies, but…"

"Travis means a lot to you, so it's a little different. No need to apologize." Sylvia cocked her head to the side. "I'm guessing you're the reason Travis has been so cranky lately. He'll barely talk about anything, and I haven't had a chance to check in with him. Did something happen?"

Janie's heart felt funny—filled with fear, but also a disconcerting openness. It was as if she was finally giving into what she'd been pushing against. She stared out into the smudgy dark sky, the stars glittering even through the haze of smoke, before she met Sylvia's gaze. "I kinda blew it. I was getting up the nerve to try to make things right and then this happened tonight."

"What do you mean you blew it?"

"I got a little freaked out and wanted some breathing room. He went and told me he thought he loved me and I forgot how to talk. That was over a week ago, and I feel like an idiot. Even worse, now I'm scared I won't even get a chance to make sure he knows how I feel. I might not be any good at this whole relationship thing, but I could've handled it a little better."

"Ah, so he did take my advice," Sylvia said softly, so softly Janie wasn't sure she heard right over the hubbub of noise around them.

"Huh?"

"Oh, I told him he should tell you how he felt. Sounds like he did."

"You told him that?"

Sylvia shrugged. "Sure. Hon, I'm old, way too old to think it's worth dancing around things like this. Maybe you didn't handle it so great, but it sounds like you might've woken up inside. Nobody said love was easy. Trust me, I've been married to Michael a long damn time. Catch me on a bad day and I still screw up." She paused, her eyes searching Janie's. "How do you feel about him?"

"Right now?"

"Yes, right now. A night like this will bring things into focus, so don't dismiss it."

Janie stared at her. Her heart was beating hard and fast—she was so afraid of what might happen, or had already happened, to Travis. Yet, through that, her feelings crystallized. She loved him. She knew that with certainty. She didn't know if she was ready, but that worry was tiny beside the depth and breadth of her feelings for him. A blast of wind gusted across the parking lot, blowing smoke and cold air across them. She held Sylvia's gaze. "I love him."

Sylvia nodded firmly. "Well, there you go. I can't promise that will give you all the answers, but at least you know that. We all have baggage, so don't go worrying about that."

Janie nodded slowly and swallowed against the

tightness in her throat. She felt buffeted by a mix of emotions—relief at being able to know her own heart, fear for Travis's immediate safety, and this gnawing anxiety that he was hurt and she couldn't get to him.

"Mom!"

Janie glanced over to see Stella hurrying over to them. She stood up. "Stella, I told you to stay in the car! What…?"

"But you promised to come tell me once you knew what was going on," Stella countered.

Janie sighed internally. She'd completely forgotten to let Stella know what was going on in the maelstrom of her worry. Stella reached them and silently handed Janie the car keys before crossing her arms and looking between them. "So?"

"Hon, we're waiting for them to find Travis and Ben," Sylvia said, her voice calm and clear. "Sit with me." She patted the table beside her.

Stella's eyes swung from Sylvia to Janie—wide with concern. Janie met her gaze, a thread of strength holding her together. "Let's hope for the best." Her voice sounded confident and hopeful, but it belied the depth of worry pounding in her heart and tying her in knots inside.

Time crept by. Minutes felt like hours. Janie kept checking her watch to find not much time had passed. Finally, there was a call from one of the hotel entrances. One of the emergency responder teams raced over to the entrance with a stretcher. Janie stood and started to move in that direction, only to have Sylvia grip her arm and hold her in place. "You can't go over there right now. Wait and see. If it's him, Darren will tell you right away. They don't need anyone else in the fire zone."

Janie closed her eyes and forced herself to stay where she was. She didn't even know if it was Travis. Logically, she knew Sylvia was right. She would be nothing but in the way if she raced over there. She paced back and forth in front of the small table. Ken had left a while ago to work with the crew and had gone into the hotel himself. The crews appeared to have gotten control of the fire. Flames were no longer streaking up into the sky. Smoke billowed from the dampened fire everywhere. The emergency crews had organized shuttles to get the guests to other nearby hotels, so there were vehicles rotating into the parking lot on the far side, out of the way of the fire crews.

Janie waited and waited to have someone come tell her if they'd found Travis. When she couldn't wait anymore, she looked to Sylvia and Stella. "I'm not going to get in the way, but I'm going over there..." she gestured to one of the ambulances out of the way "...and find out if that's Travis."

She didn't wait for Sylvia's reply and jogged over there quickly. Her heart sank when the EMT waiting by the ambulance reported the person brought out of the building was Ben. With her arms wrapped around her waist and hot tears rolling down her cheeks, she trudged back toward where Sylvia and Stella were waiting. She stopped before she got too close and tried to gather herself. She didn't want to cry in front of Stella, not right now. She looked up into the sky and let the icy air dry her tears. Swallowing down her fear, she gave herself a shake and kept walking.

They both looked to her and didn't say a word. She knew they knew that it clearly wasn't Travis on the stretcher. While she was relieved to know Ben was safe and sound, the heart crushing worry she felt wouldn't dissipate until she knew Travis was out of harm's way. Time kept crawling by. When she heard another call from the wing furthest away, she stood again and watched while another crew raced to the entrance. An ambulance carrying Ben had left already. She didn't give Sylvia a chance to grab her arm this time. She called over her shoulder as she raced off. "I'll stay out of the way!"

She kept her word and stopped at a distance by one of the ambulances. All she could see was the cluster of firefighters surrounding whoever was being placed on a stretcher. The three men carrying the stretcher broke free and aimed directly for the ambulance.

"Janie."

Startled, she jumped and looked to her side to find Darren right there. "Why don't you ride with me to the hospital?" he asked.

She shook her head. "No. I want to see Travis. I'll ride with him in the ambulance."

Darren looked away and nodded abruptly. "Fine. He doesn't look so good, okay? I just want you to be prepared."

"Will he be okay?" she asked, shaky inside with her heart hammering away.

"As best as I can guess, probably. Sounds like a beam fell and he broke his leg. He sustained some injuries almost everywhere you can see and his face is bloodied."

On the heels of the rushing relief at hearing Travis might be okay came a crashing wave of concern. With her heart racing, she waited with Darren by the ambulance. Only when the stretcher was close did she break away and race over. Travis was covered in soot, his gear blackened and dark steaks mingling with the blood on his face. His firefighter gear was so heavy that she couldn't ascertain any injuries other than his face. She reached the stretcher and looked down. His eyes were closed and his forehead furrowed with pain.

The EMT's, all of whom were unfamiliar to her so she figured they must be one of the crews from out of town, glanced at her and kept moving. They rolled a cart out and lifted the stretcher onto it. She curled her hands on the rail and looked for where she could touch Travis, finally settling to curl her hand over his where it rested on the stretcher. His eyes opened.

"Hey," she said because that was about all she could manage. She fought against the tears, but one escaped and rolled down her cheek.

He started to shake his head, but grimaced the second he tried to move. She squeezed his hand. He held her eyes. "I'm okay, just a little banged up. Think I might need to borrow Stella's crutches." He managed to crack a smile through the soot and blood streaking his face. His attempt at humor sent a wave of emotion cresting inside and she swallowed against the tears.

For a moment, she was jostled out of the way. Darren interjected to let the ambulance crew know she had requested to ride with Travis to the hospital. She released his hand as they got the stretcher into the ambulance. An EMT with an easy-going smile held out a hand and lifted her into the back of the ambulance. Once she was seated beside Travis, the man spoke. "He's a bit worse for the wear, but he'll be all right. I'm Evan by the way."

"You think he'll be okay?" she asked, too worried

about Travis's state to introduce herself in return.

"Oh, setting that leg break will be hell, but after that, he'll be okay."

Travis started to chuckle and grimaced again. "Think I must've broken a rib too."

"Well then, that'll hurt worse than your leg," Evan said with a shrug.

Evan got busy hooking Travis up to a monitor and checking his blood pressure. He chatted casually with the driver, leaving Janie to keep her eyes pinned to Travis. Her heart felt cracked open, emotions pouring out inside. She gulped in air, trying to get a handle on herself. Travis asked Evan a few questions, but she didn't hear a thing he said. When he looked her way again, he gave her hand a squeeze. "Don't look like that. I'll be fine. Just a little banged up."

"I love you," she blurted out, tears rolling down her cheeks. "I didn't mean to be such an idiot last week. I got all messed up in my head and…"

He squeezed her hand again. "Hey, hey. You didn't mess up. It's not like I handled it that great. I showed up and dumped it all on you." He freed his hand from hers and lifted it to knuckle her tears away. "Love you too."

His words were raspy from the smoke. She scrambled inside to contain her emotions and tried to stop crying, but the tears kept rolling down her cheeks. He curled his hand over hers and held on through the last few minutes of the ride, which were busy with Evan adjusting a few things hooked up to Travis and checking to make sure his leg was stationary. When they arrived at the hospital, Travis was whisked away.

"I'll be waiting right here," she said as he was wheeled away.

CHAPTER 21

ravis slowly came awake. He didn't remember much from last night after he got to the hospital beyond the doctor telling him he wouldn't need surgery. He opened his eyes and rolled his head to the side to find he was in Janie's bedroom. She wasn't in bed with him, but he could hear the shower running. He carefully moved his leg and was relieved to discover he wasn't in too much pain. He was sore from head to toe and had a dull pain in his leg. He lifted the covers to see he had a cast up to his knee. He took a deep breath and felt a twinge in his ribs. It was as if he was on an expedition to figure out the extent of his injuries. He had bandaging across his ribs on his right side, along with the cast on his lower right leg. His memories of being inside the hotel were much clearer. He'd just finished escorting a family to the stairwell when he heard something. He'd headed back down the hall, barely able to see through the smoke, and a beam crashed down from the ceiling. He'd managed to roll and get out of the way, but he'd fallen on his right side, likely cracking his ribs and breaking his ankle at once. The beam had pinned his ankle, trapping him in place.

It had been a long wait for the crew to find him. The hotel was sprawling with long hallways. Trying to keep his mind off his precarious situation, his thoughts had circled back to Janie over and over again. By the time he was carried out, the relief he felt at seeing her had been immense. A sense of elation mingled with relief rose inside when he recalled her telling him she loved him. He might not remember much after that, but those words were crystal clear in his mind and heart. The water stopped running, and he pushed himself up, propping the pillows up behind him. He leaned back with a sigh just as Janie stepped out of the bathroom.

She wore a fluffy green robe. Her damp hair hung about her shoulders, and her skin was flushed from her shower. One look at her, no matter his battered state, and a jolt of lust shot through him. She froze where she was, her eyes locking with his. A long week without her and seeing her felt so damn good, he wanted to grab her and yank her into his arms. He held a hand out, beckoning her to his side. As she walked to the bed, the air between them hummed, alive with the current of their connection.

She sat down on the edge of the bed, lacing her fingers into his. "How do you feel?"

"Fine. Don't remember a damn thing after I got to the hospital, except the doctor saying I wouldn't need surgery. What happened after that?"

Her eyes skated over him, sending little jolts through him. All he wanted was her. Now. Damn his condition. "Well, they gave you a sedative before they set your leg. They cleaned you up and turned you over to me. I guess you don't remember me, Stella and my mom hauling you inside, huh?"

He chuckled and shook his head. Her eyes were worried and kept scanning him. "You sure you feel okay?"

"I'm a little sore. I'm sure it won't be good for me to laugh too hard, or put any weight on my right leg, but all in all, I feel fine. Stop looking at me like that." He didn't like seeing her worried, although a part of him soaked it up.

Her eyes narrowed. "You were trapped in a fire and had a beam fall on you! I get to be worried."

His heart skipped a beat, and he squeezed her hand. "Okay, be worried, but I feel fine. I'll be sore and my ribs will annoy the hell outta me, but once I'm off the crutches, I'll be back to normal."

Her eyes held his, her gaze softening. She squeezed his hand in return. "I know. Last night was…hard. I was so scared and so worried, and it felt like forever."

He released her hand and reached up to brush a damp lock of hair away from her face. "I know. Let's not dwell on it. Like I said, I'm a little banged up, but otherwise good."

He couldn't resist trailing his fingertip along the soft, flushed skin of her neck. He followed the edge of her robe, tracing her collarbone and into the valley between her breasts. He didn't much care for anything other than to touch as much of her as he could right now. When he slipped his hand under the edge of her robe to trace her nipple, her breath drew in sharply.

"Stop it! You are in no shape for this…" Her words

trailed off on a gasp when he lightly pinched her nipple.

He saw the dark passion flickering in her gaze even as she shook her head and started to move away. He didn't give her a chance to pull away. He reached for her and pulled her into his lap. He might not have the finesse to do it smoothly at the moment, but she was in his lap. A bundle of soft curves, her skin dewy from the shower and so tempting, he ignored her protests and dipped his head to start a trail of wet kisses into the valley between her breasts. When she shifted in his lap, her robe got caught on her knee and a breast popped out. He glanced up through his lashes before swirling his tongue around her nipple and biting down softly. At her sharp cry, he smiled against her skin before leaning back.

He could feel the wet heat of her against his rock-hard cock. The thin cotton of his briefs was the slightest deterrent. She'd ended up straddling him, which he didn't think she'd intended when he yanked her into his lap, but it worked for him. She was completely bare under her robe, and damn was he pleased about that. Oblivious to the dull pain in his leg and ignoring the twinges in his ribs, he pushed her robe off her shoulders and cupped her breasts, dragging his thumbs back and forth over her taut nipples.

"Travis…" his name came out on a husky sigh. "We can't do this." She started to wiggle away, which only served to create friction between them.

He arched into her and grinned when her lips parted and a low moan escaped. "Sure we can. All we have to do is…" He paused to drag his hand down over her abdomen and sift through her curls to her slick folds. She was hot, wet and ready no matter what she said. "This," he said as he slid one finger and then another into her channel.

Her eyes fell closed and her hips rolled into his touch. He tangled his free hand in her hair and pulled her down for a kiss. She didn't resist, her lips coming against his swiftly. He poured himself into their kiss—licks, strokes, nips and kisses. He couldn't get enough. All the while, he plunged his fingers into her channel again and again and again. She abruptly tore her lips away. Her body nearly vibrated around him. "If we're doing this, I want to feel you inside of me," she said, her words breathy.

He wasn't about to argue. She pointed a finger at him. "Don't you move. Let me do the work," she ordered.

Fine by him. She shimmied her hips back, and he regretfully let his fingers slide out of her. She curled her hand over his cock, giving it a rough stroke over his briefs. He was so ready, he almost came right then and there. He latched onto his control and held on as she carefully dragged his briefs down, just far enough for his cock to spring free. He had to fight to hold still. The truth was, even if he wanted to move much, he really couldn't. Not with his leg and ribs. With her straddling him, he could manage all of this, but anything else and he'd end up on the floor.

She dipped her head and dragged her tongue along each side of his cock before taking him fully into her mouth. Holy hell. Her mouth worked him like magic until he was so close to the edge, he cried her name hoarsely. She lifted her head and rose up over him. He suddenly recalled he had no idea where his clothes were and had no clue if there was a condom anywhere in the vicinity. He closed his eyes and gritted his teeth. "Wait."

Opening his eyes, he found hers on him, dark with passion and need. It took all of his discipline to speak. "I don't even know if I have a condom here," he choked out.

"It's okay. I started the pill a while ago. I didn't want to have to worry, so..." She flushed and lifted a shoulder in a shrug. "If it's okay..."

"Oh, it's more than okay," he said with alacrity.

She reached between them and guided him to her entrance. She held still for a long moment, teasing him with her wet heat, before she sank down deeply, seating herself against him and bringing him fully inside of her. His eyes fell closed and he groaned, nearly drunk at how good it was to feel her without any barriers between them.

* * *

TRAVIS STROKED a palm up her spine, bringing her closer to him as she started to slowly rock her hips against his. Already verging on a climax, Janie bit her lip and tried to corral the wild pleasure tearing through her. It felt so good—so, so good—to have his hot length filling and stretching her. She hadn't realized how desperate she was to be this close to him until he touched her. It was as if she'd been parched of thirst and a drop of water fell. Now, she couldn't get enough and soaked in every subtle touch—where their skin slid together as they rocked, the heat of his hand on her back, his lips trailing kisses along her neck, and him rocking deeper and deeper into her with each moment.

"Janie."

She opened her eyes and collided with the blur of his blue gaze. He reached between them and barely dragged his thumb across her clit, right where they were joined. That was it. Pleasure burst through her with such force, tremors wracked her. His cry joined hers as his body tightened. She felt his release inside. His hand slid down her back and his head fell forward, resting between her breasts. She resisted the urge to collapse against him, mindful that she might've lost her mind and allowed this with him injured, but she wasn't going to make matters worse.

She stroked a hand through his hair, a wave of emotion rolling through her. She was so relieved he was safe, so relieved to know he just needed some time to heal, and so relieved to be this close to him again—right where she belonged. He lifted his head. "I love you," he said, his voice gruff.

Tears were hot against the back of her eyes. She swallowed against the tightness in her throat and dipped her head to catch his lips in a kiss. "Love you too," she murmured against his lips.

* * *

A WHILE LATER, after Janie made sure Travis got in and out of the shower safely and helped him down the stairs, they found Stella waiting in the kitchen.

"You made coffee!" Janie said, throwing a grin Stella's way.

Stella grinned. "Yup. I knew you'd run down here and make it right away, so I figured I'd have it ready. I also have batter ready for pancakes."

Travis had stopped by the foot of the stairs, his

hand on the railing. "Well, damn. All I had to do was break my leg to get you to make breakfast."

Stella burst out laughing and stood up from the stool by the counter. "Here. Let me show you how to use your crutches."

She picked up the crutches they'd carted home from the hospital last night and left by the door. Janie poured coffee for her and Travis and slipped onto a stool by the counter to watch. Travis gamely went along with Stella's guidance and crutched his way in a circle around the living room. "Are these the same crutches you were using?" he asked once he made his way back to the kitchen.

Stella shook her head. "Nope. They said mine would be too small."

Travis reached the counter and eased onto a stool across from Janie. A glimmer of pain flashed in his eyes.

"Why don't we get you settled on the couch?" Janie asked as she stood, hurrying to help.

He waved her away. "Nope. My ribs are sore, that's all." He stretched his leg out to the side and reached out to squeeze her hand quickly. "Seriously. I'm fine."

She returned to sit across from him and slid his mug of coffee over. The morning passed in a warm blur. Stella insisted on making pancakes without any help and gleefully served them breakfast. After they ate, Stella bossed Travis into resting on the couch. They spent the rest of the morning watching television and relaxing.

Janie went upstairs to get dressed late that morning and stared at herself in the mirror. She could hear Stella bantering with Travis about something, and her heart did a little flip. She'd never allowed herself to imagine a lazy morning like this. Not one that included a man who made her feel like no one else had ever made her feel. Her reflection stared back at her—her features relaxed and those familiar lines of tension gone. Starting her day with a bone-melting climax seemed to set a good tone.

CHAPTER 22

On Christmas Eve, Travis crutched his way up the steps to Janie's house. The kitchen door swung open, and Stella stood in the doorway, grinning like mad. Pansy dashed past her and bounded into the snow. By the time he made it through the doorway, Pansy was racing back inside.

"Hey Travis! Mom called to say she's running late."

He crutched his way past Stella into the kitchen. "Thanks for letting me in anyway," he said with a grin.

Stella closed the door behind him while Pansy shook herself and sent the snow dusting her fur in an arc around her. "As if I'd make you wait outside," Stella said with a roll of her eyes. She spun to the counter and immediately picked up her phone and started texting.

Travis crutched his way to the couch and eased down, his eyes landing on the Christmas tree in the corner. Pansy had done a little damage to one corner with the branches ragged and torn. Presents were piled high underneath, and the lights strung along the ceiling brightened the room. He couldn't wait until he got his cast off, but in the meantime, he was making do. It was the least of his reasons for being ecstatic about finally breaking through the walls around Janie's heart, but he found it quite convenient that she wanted to fuss over him all the time. As such, she'd refused to let him stay at his apartment, insisting he shouldn't be alone right now. He watched while Stella walked upstairs, her eyes intent on her phone.

She'd survived the anticipation of the Christmas Dance and returned home jubilant from actually enjoying herself. After meeting Parker more than in passing, Travis was confident Parker liked Stella as much more than a friend. He'd shared as much with Janie, and she'd burst out laughing. "Oh yeah. I'm staying out of it and letting them figure it out."

Janie came swirling through the door, a whoosh of icy air blowing in with her. "Hey!" she called in his direction as she plunked several bags of groceries on the counter. He started to get up, thinking he needed to help. She turned to him with a hand on her hip. "You're not seriously trying to get up and help me right now, are you?"

"Well, yeah."

"Don't be dumb. There's nothing left to carry. Stay right there," she ordered with a wag of her finger.

He fought the annoyance rising inside, not with her, but with his limited mobility. Moments later, after she'd whirled around the kitchen, she walked over and handed him a beer. She set a glass of wine down on the coffee table and adjusted the ottoman where his casted leg was resting. "Need anything else?"

He took a long swallow of beer. "Not a thing."

"Are you hungry?"

"Nope. Stopped by the station earlier and there was food everywhere. I figure I'm better off if I don't eat much more since I'll eat plenty tomorrow."

Janie nodded and leaned back into the cushions. Stella must've started a fire not too long ago because flames were still flickering in the fireplace. Travis looked at Janie and rested his hand on the back of the couch, sifting through her glossy hair. She rolled her head to the side, her eyes catching his.

"You ready for Christmas with my family tomorrow?" she asked softly.

"Absolutely. Anything that means I get a whole day with you is awesome."

Her cheeks flushed, and she leaned forward to snag her wine and take a gulp. He was finding it ridiculously easy to adjust to the new state of being obsessed with all things Janie. She made it easy because she was, well, she was Janie. He was finding, however, that while Janie seemed to have come to terms with her feelings for him, she flushed whenever he was this direct with her. Still stroking his fingers through her hair, he watched her. "What is it?" he asked.

"What's what?" she countered.

"Whenever I say things like that, you get…like this," he gestured to her as she took another gulp of wine.

She stared at him and sighed. "I dunno. I'm not used to anyone talking to me like that. It's…new. That's all."

She leaned forward and traced the edge of his jaw. "I might not be used to it, but I like it," she said, her voice husky as she brought her lips to his.

Not much later, Janie flicked off the lights in the living room. The room fell into darkness. She turned to face him, and he realized the sky was lit up behind her in the windows. He grabbed his crutches and stood quickly. "Look!" He gestured toward the windows with the bottom of one of his crutches.

She spun around, and he heard her breath catch. "Oh, I love the northern lights! I haven't seen any yet this winter."

She stepped closer to the windows. He made his way to her and leaned against the wall by the windows, reaching for her and pulling her against his side. They stood in the darkened room and watched the colors dance across the sky. Shades of purple, blue and green in varying intensity rippled through the darkness. Only when the colors started to fade did Janie shift. He experienced a tiny pang of loss when her soft warmth moved away. "Let's go upstairs," she whispered.

Once he clomped upstairs and managed to get in bed, Janie slipped under the covers beside him. He had a clear view of the sky over the bay. With Janie's lush body curled up against his, he felt relaxed to his core. He watched the northern lights slowly fade into the darkness as her breathing evened into sleep. He'd never have thought falling asleep beside someone could feel this way, but right here, right now, he felt better than he ever had. Given he had a bum leg in a cast and his ribs were still sore as hell, that was saying something.

* * *

"MOM!"

Janie was just standing up from the oven as she carefully removed the turkey. She set it down on the stove and turned as Stella slid across the kitchen in her socked feet. "There's just no way to get you to remember you're supposed to take it easy for another few weeks with that ankle, is there?" Janie asked with a shake of her head.

Stella grinned. "I'm fine. I'm not running or jumping up and down. Anyway, you should be worried about Travis now, not me."

Janie chuckled. "Right. Anyway, what's up?"

"Can Parker come over later?"

"Let me talk to his mom first."

"Why? You don't usually say you have to talk to her first."

"Usually not, but it's Christmas Day. I know you want to see him, but I need to make sure it's okay with his parents if he's not there for a little bit today."

Stella's shoulders fell in an exaggerated droop, but she sighed and nodded. "Will you call her now?"

"Give me five minutes."

Janie watched Stella meander out of the kitchen, grabbing a piece of cheese off of a tray on the counter as she passed by. Their house was filled with her family...and Travis. At the moment, he was seated in the corner of the couch with his leg propped up on an ottoman. Her mother and her two aunts, Pam and Sharon, were helping her in the kitchen, while her uncle Cody and Stella's four cousins were scattered around the house between the living room and the sunroom. A football game was on television and Travis was bantering with her uncle about something to do with sports. She should've guessed he already knew almost everyone in her family. Apparently, he'd crewed with her uncle on the Winters' brothers commercial crew a few summers ago.

Travis glanced her way, his eyes catching hers. One look and it was as if a flame lit the air between them. Heat suffused her and her low belly clenched. She had to remind herself they were surrounded by family and tear her eyes away to focus on something other than him. "Hon, I'm starting the gravy," her mother said from over her shoulder.

Janie wiped her hands on a towel and slipped her phone out of her pocket. "Perfect. I'll be right back. Need to make a call."

After she checked with Parker's mother and got the green light for him to visit for a few hours this evening, she returned to the kitchen. Before she knew it, they were sitting down to eat. In her family, that wasn't a formal affair. Although she had a dining table to one side of the kitchen, they'd elected to use it as a buffet table for serving and to eat scattered about the living room. There were just enough people here for the table to be crowded. Travis tried to insist he could serve himself, but after he almost dropped a plate while attempting to juggle his crutches and the plate, Janie elbowed him out of the way.

"Back to the couch. Tell me what you want, and I'll take care of it."

He dipped his head and dropped a lingering kiss in the curve of her neck, sending a hot shiver through her. When he lifted his head, her breath caught. Again, she had to remind herself where they were. "I'm not picky. Just get me some of everything," he said, the low timbre of his voice sending another shiver over her skin.

He crutched his way back to the couch, while she

tried to focus and get their plates filled. Hours later, she wiped down the kitchen counter and turned on the dishwasher. Her family members had gradually left with her mother being the last hold out as she insisted everything get put away first. Parker had practically had to be shoved out the door. Janie was fairly certain he and Stella had managed to sneak in a few kisses in the sunroom. She hung the dishtowel on the oven handle and glanced to Travis. He was back in the corner of the couch with his foot propped up. The fire was dying down with embers glowing in the dim light. She closed her eyes and took a deep breath. Her heart felt so full.

She walked to the couch and settled into the cushions beside Travis. He curled his arm over her shoulders and pulled her against him. Even now, tired from a long day of cooking and the buzz of company all day, the feel of his muscled body against hers set a hum to life inside of her. She wondered if she'd ever get used to it. She relaxed against him and glanced up. Tracing a fingertip along his stubbled jaw, she smiled softly. "Well, you survived."

His shoulders shook with his laughter before he pinned her with his gaze. "You need to stop worrying any of this is hard for me. Aside from the fact your family's pretty easy to be around, none of it really matters. The only thing that matters about today was I got to spend it with you."

A rush of emotion welled inside. He sifted his fingers through her hair and angled his head down, catching her lips in a quick kiss.

*T*ravis walked down the dock at Otter Cove Harbor, weary from a long afternoon helping Nathan get their boat ready to be pulled from the harbor tomorrow. Nathan had left a few minutes earlier when Travis had realized he'd left his backpack on the boat. He was looking down when he heard his name and glanced up to see Janie jogging down the docks to meet him. He smiled inside and out—the kind of smile only she could elicit. She reached him finally and threw her arms around his neck. "Stella just got accepted to the music program at UW!"

He held her fast against him and leaned his head back. "Awesome!"

Janie kissed him quickly and wiggled, shimmying out of his hold. She slipped her hand in his and walked alongside him. "She's beside herself. I promised we'd take her out for pizza."

"Of course. Let me get home and clean up first. I'm guessing she'll want to bring Parker."

Janie grinned up at him. "Of course. He's in the

same program, so I'm trying to decide if it's best to just accept that they'll probably move in together."

He couldn't help but laugh. "It is what it is. Whatever happens, Stella will be fine. Parker's a good guy. I'm not worried I'll have to threaten to kick his ass or anything."

Janie held his gaze for a long moment and then nodded firmly. He'd discovered over the last year that he loved how she'd come to look for him for advice. He couldn't quite believe it, but they were a team when it came to parenting. When he'd moved in early last spring, he hadn't known how that part of their relationship would play out. She'd quickly looped him into the dynamic and seemed beyond relieved for back up with some of the challenging issues. Stella was pretty well-behaved, but she was a teenager with a bumpy history. She had her moments and even her days, but all in all, they got through it.

As they walked down the docks, he scanned the view. It was late afternoon on a chilly winter day. The sky was dotted with clouds, and wind was gusting across the bay. The mountains were tall and majestic on the far side, their snow-tipped peaks stark against the sky. A gust of wind blew Janie's hair in a swirl. He glanced down and caught sight of the ring on her hand—a simple platinum band. He'd hemmed and hawed over his proposal and eventually sought Stella's advice. She'd bluntly told him Janie wasn't much of a fan of stones because then she had to worry about them. After all of his worries, Janie had surprised him by bursting into tears and flinging herself at him when he'd asked her to marry him. They'd had a simple ceremony this past summer. He still marveled every day when he woke up beside her and shrugged off the teasing at work over how quickly he'd gone from being a bachelor to a family man.

He gave Janie's hand a squeeze and stopped her on the docks. She glanced up, those hazel eyes—layers of color he lost himself in time and again—locked to his. "What?"

"Just this…"

He leaned down and brought his lips to hers. They were warm in the cold air.

* * *

JANIE LEANED back in the booth and sighed. She pushed her plate away and eyed the pizza in the center of the table. They were at Glacier Pizza, and Travis's arm was draped across her shoulders, his thumb idly stroking along her collarbone and distracting her. He distracted her almost all the time, but she'd become accustomed to it. He was laughing at something Stella said.

Stella snagged the last piece of pizza and took a bite, her dark brown eyes bouncing to Janie. "Thanks for taking me out for pizza."

Janie grinned. "Of course! You got some awesome news."

Stella's eyes flicked to Travis, her smile expanding. "This is so perfect! You guys figured it out in time."

Travis took a swig of his beer and cocked his head to the side. "Huh?"

Stella waved her free hand between them, still nibbling on the piece of pizza held in her other hand. "You fell in love and got married. I know Mom would've been fine no matter what, but she's a people person. It took you to get her to wake up and stop being all to herself all the time."

Travis nodded slowly. "The falling in love part was easy." He gave Janie's shoulder a squeeze. "Your mom was just fine without me, so I consider myself lucky."

Stella said something else and the conversation moved on. Janie's mind spun back to the years before she'd locked eyes with Travis. She'd come to realize she'd let old Randy have far more influence on her than she'd ever wanted. Randy's dramatic entrance back into Diamond Creek had ended with a whimper when he worked out a plea deal for his charges. As it was, the best deal he could get meant fifteen years behind bars because of his long history and the felony assault charges. Janie felt truly free of the hold his violence had on her.

A while later, she walked beside Travis onto the back deck at the house. Stella had bounded up to her room to 'talk' to Parker, which meant some combination of texting and screen time on their phones. Christmas was days away, and she couldn't quite believe this would be her second Christmas with Travis. With Stella's insistence, they'd gone all out with decorating this year. Travis had helped Stella hang lights along the roof and on a number of spruce trees in the yard, creating a magical feeling outside in the cold darkness. They stopped by the railing, and she looked up into the sky. "Oh! Northern lights," she said on a breath.

Travis glanced up, following where she pointed. Just above the mountains across the bay, the faintest glimmer of green and blue rippled in the dark sky. As they stood in the quiet, the colors deepened in intensity, moving like a curtain in the darkness. A shimmer of color come to life. The water in the bay reflected the colors back up. Travis stepped behind her and slipped his arms around her waist. She leaned into his warmth and strength. They remained like that while the lights gave a show—surreal and mesmerizing.

She didn't realize she was getting cold until she shivered. He tightened his arms around her. He dipped his head into the curve of her neck, his lips a searing warmth in the icy cold.

Thank you for reading Christmas Nights - I hope you loved Travis & Janie's story!

For more swoony & sassy romance...

This Crazy Love kicks off the Swoon Series - small town southern romance with enough heat to melt you! Jackson & Shay's story is epic - swoon-worthy & intensely emotional. Jackson just happens to be Shay's brother's best friend. He's also *seriously* easy on the eyes. Shay has a past, the kind of past she would most definitely like to forget. Past or not, Jackson is about to rock her world. Don't miss their story! Free on all retailers!

Burn For Me is a second chance romance for the ages. Sexy firefighters? Check. Rugged men? Check. Wrapped up together? Check. Brave the fire in this hot, small-town romance. Amelia & Cade were high school sweethearts & then it all fell apart. When they cross paths again, it's epic - don't miss Cade's story! Free on all retailers!

For more small town romance, take a visit to Last Frontier Lodge in Diamond Creek. A sexy, alpha SEAL meets his match with a brainy heroine in Take Me Home. Marley is all brains & Gage is all brawn. Sparks fly when their worlds collide. Don't miss Gage & Marley's story!
Free on all retailers!

If sports romance lights your spark, check out The Play. Liam is a British footballer who falls for Olivia, his doctor. A twist of forbidden heats up this swoon-worthy & laugh-out-loud romance. Don't miss Liam & Olivia's story.
Free on all retailers!

Be sure to sign up for my newsletter for the latest news, teasers & more! Click here to sign up: http://jhcroixauthor.com/subscribe/

FIND MY BOOKS

Thank you for reading Christmas Nights! I hope you enjoyed the story. If so, you can help other readers find my books in a variety of ways.

1) Write a review!

2) Sign up for my newsletter, so you can receive information about upcoming new releases & receive a FREE copy of one of my books: http://jhcroixauthor.com/subscribe/

3) Like and follow my Amazon Author page at https://amazon.com/author/jhcroix

4) Follow me on Bookbub at https://www.bookbub.com/authors/j-h-croix

5) Follow me on Twitter at https://twitter.com/JHCroix

6) Like my Facebook page at https://www.facebook.com/jhcroix

* * *

Visit my store to purchase ebooks & fun swag!

J.H. Croix Shop

Diamond Creek Alaska Novels
When Love Comes
Follow Love
Love Unbroken
Love Untamed
Tumble Into Love
Christmas Nights
Last Frontier Lodge Novels
Take Me Home
Love at Last
Just This Once
Falling Fast
Stay With Me
When We Fall
Hold Me Close
Crazy For You
Just Us
Fireweed Harbor Series
When We Meet - free prequel!
Make You Mine
Dare To Fall - due out June 2023!
Be The One - due out October 2023!
Light My Fire Series
Wild With You
Hold Me Now
Only Ever Us
Fall For Me
Keep Me Close
With Every Breath
All It Takes
Take Me Now - due out August 2023!
Dare With Me Series

Crash Into You
Evers & Afters
Come To Me
Back To Us
Take Me There
After We Fall
Swoon Series
This Crazy Love
Wait For Me
Break My Fall
Truly Madly Mine
Still Go Crazy
If We Dare
Steal My Heart
Into The Fire Series
Burn For Me
Slow Burn
Burn So Bad
Hot Mess
Burn So Good
Sweet Fire
Play With Fire
Melt With You
Burn For You
Crash & Burn
That Snowy Night
Brit Boys Sports Romance
The Play
Big Win
Out Of Bounds
Play Me
Naughty Wish

ACKNOWLEDGMENTS

To my readers who kept asking when Travis would get his story - this one's for you! No story would make it to the end without my editor making sure each character gets my best. This cover is gorgeous because Clarise Tan at CT Cover Creations is just that magical! Last, but never least…the man who reminds me love is about laughter.

xoxo

J.H. Croix

ABOUT THE AUTHOR

USA Today Bestselling Author J.H. Croix lives in a small town in Maine with her husband and two spoiled dogs. Croix writes contemporary romance with sassy women and alpha men who aren't afraid to show some emotion. Her love for quirky small-towns and the characters that inhabit them shines through in her writing. Take a walk on the wild side of romance with her bestselling novels!

Places you can find me:
jhcroixauthor.com
jhcroix@jhcroix.com

facebook.com/jhcroix
instagram.com/jhcroix
bookbub.com/authors/j-h-croix